HAUNTED
THE GHOST ON THE STAIRS

HAUNTED
THE GHOST ON THE STAIRS

CHRIS EBOCH

ALADDIN
NEW YORK LONDON TORONTO SYDNEY

FOR THE CRITIQUERS

This book is a work of fiction. Any references to historical events, real people, or real locales are used fictitiously. Other names, characters, places, and incidents are the product of the author's imagination, and any resemblance to actual events or locales or persons, living or dead, is entirely coincidental.

ALADDIN

An imprint of Simon & Schuster Children's Publishing Division

1230 Avenue of the Americas, New York, NY 10020

First Aladdin paperback edition August 2009

Text copyright © 2009 by Chris Eboch

All rights reserved, including the right of reproduction in whole or in part in any form.

ALADDIN is a trademark of Simon & Schuster, Inc., and related logo is a registered trademark of Simon & Schuster, Inc.

For information about special discounts for bulk purchases, please contact Simon & Schuster Special Sales at 1-866-506-1949 or business@simonandschuster.com. The Simon & Schuster Speakers Bureau can bring authors to your live event. For more information or to book an event contact the Simon & Schuster Speakers Bureau at 1-866-248-3049 or visit our website at www.simonspeakers.com.

Designed by Ann Zeak and Lisa Vega

The text of this book was set in Minister Std.

Manufactured in the United States of America

10 9 8 7 6 5 4 3 2 1

Library of Congress Control Number 2008934661

ISBN 978-1-4169-7548-9   ISBN 978-1-4169-9627-9 (eBook)

ACKNOWLEDGMENTS

Many thanks to my critique partners for your support and insight: Rollin Thomas, Ralph Neighbor, Gail Martini-Peterson, Barbara Parker, Marjorie Watkins, and especially David West for pushing me farther and David Rogers for keeping it real. Thanks also to my brother, Doug Eboch, for help with the TV show, and to Mark McVeigh and Alyson Heller for bringing this series to life.

CHAPTER
1

don't like it," Tania said.

I glanced down at my sister, then back at the hotel. "It looks like an old castle."

"It *looks* haunted."

I laughed. "Don't tell me you're starting to believe that garbage!"

She hunched her head between her shoulders. "Of course not. I just mean it's spooky."

"You just feel that way because . . . because of everything that's happened."

She kept staring at the hotel, her blue eyes huge in her thin face. She was standing so close, I could smell her peppermint shampoo. I wasn't sure what to say to Tania sometimes. We'd gotten pretty close in the last two years, even though she was my little sister. Nobody else understood what we had been through. But what did I know about eleven-year-old girls? And knowing what she had been through, I knew I couldn't say anything to make things better. Still, I was her big brother and had to try.

The hotel really did look like a castle, with tall, narrow windows in gray stone walls. The top of the wall had notches in it—crenellations, I think they're called. A gargoyle squatted above the door, sticking his tongue out at us. They must have modeled the hotel on something in Europe, because it sure didn't look American, even though we were in Colorado.

I said, "It's four stars, and we have our own rooms. Mom and Bruce will be so busy with their TV show that we can do anything we want. We can order room service and watch cable all day. Or we can explore, and they'll let us go anywhere, because we're with the TV crew. It'll be cool."

She finally looked up at me, and managed a little smile. I grinned at her.

"Jonathan! Titania!" Our mother waved from near the camera crew's van. "Come here, I want you to meet someone."

Tania's nose wrinkled. I crossed my eyes at her, and we walked to the van with Tania sticking as close as a Siamese twin.

This girl stepped out of the van. My heart jumped into my throat.

Mom said, "This is Magdalene, the production assistant. She'll look after you, so ask her if you need anything."

I stepped away from Tania, but she scooted right up next to me again. My voice squeaked as I said "Hi!" and I felt my face get hot. I thrust out my hand and tried to lower my voice. I stammered, "I'm, um, it's nice to meet you."

She took my hand for about half a second and said, "Call me Maggie." Her eyes flicked from Tania to me. I tried to think of something to say, but my brain wasn't working. She turned and crawled back into the van.

Mom said, "Go on into the hotel. Bruce will give you your room keys."

I lingered to see if Maggie would come back out of the van. Tania took half a step away, and then turned and looked back. "Jon?" I sighed and followed her, glancing over my shoulder.

I trailed through the door after Tania. Just inside, I stopped to look around. Sure enough, a suit of armor stood next to the curving staircase ahead of us. "Man, where do they think they are?" I whispered. "And when?"

Tania gasped. I glanced at her to see where she was looking. She was staring straight ahead, with her mouth open. I couldn't see anything so interesting on the stairs.

I looked back out the door toward the van. What was Maggie doing? Could I help?

Tania made some sound. "What's up?" I mumbled.

I heard a thump and looked back to see Tania crumpled on the floor.

CHAPTER

2

I paced the small living room of the suite Tania and I would share, listening to the low voices from Tania's bedroom. I felt awful about her fall. I mean, she was right next to me. If I'd been paying attention, I could have caught her before she hit the floor.

Finally Mom came out, clutching the doctor's arm and scurrying alongside him. "Are you sure?" she whispered. "You're absolutely sure?"

He sighed. "Have your doctor do a complete blood workup when you get home, if you're worried. But it looks to me like a simple matter of low blood sugar and too much excitement. She said she didn't eat much breakfast. Order something from room service, and she'll be fine in a few hours."

He paused by the door and gently pried Mom's hand off his arm. "Remember, she's starting puberty. Her body's changing, and it will take her a while to get used to it. Just make sure she eats enough."

He slipped out, and Mom stood blinking after him. She turned back to me, her face creased with worry. "You heard what he said? Everything will be all right. Oh, Jon, I don't know what to do! I don't want to leave her, but Bruce will be waiting, and the TV people. There's so much to do."

I sighed. Whenever Tania or I got the slightest cold or skinned knee, Mom went into a panic and drove us nuts. We didn't need Mom hanging around all day, fussing at us. Anyway, I owed Tania a favor for letting her fall. "You go ahead. I'll stay with Tania."

"Really, darling? I hate to ask you to stay in your room all afternoon on your first day here, but . . . it would be such a help."

"No problem."

She hugged me tight. Her head only came up to my nose, but she squeezed so hard, I could barely breathe. She wasn't trying to comfort me—she was the one who needed comfort. I didn't have to be a genius to figure that out. She'd lost one child; she couldn't stand the thought of losing another. My own stomach was tight with worry. But I smiled and promised to order a whole banquet from room service.

I finally got Mom out the door. She looked back

and said, "Don't let anything happen to her."

Nice. Not too much responsibility. I smiled and kept my voice steady. "I won't."

Tania was sitting in bed, propped up with about five giant pillows. She looked tiny and pale in the big bed with its bright red and gold cover. She glanced up at me and then quickly looked down at her hands. Her pale hair swung in front of her face.

I sat in the chair next to the bed. I cleared my throat. "How are you feeling?"

She didn't look up as she whispered, "All right."

She was mad at me. I said, "I'm sorry. Really, really sorry—I mean it."

She looked at me then, her eyes wide. "Sorry? What for?"

"For letting you fall! You were right next to me and I should have caught you."

She shrugged. "Oh, that. It doesn't matter."

I stared at her. Something was bothering her, but what? She looked down again, and I could just see her cheeks getting red through her fringe of hair. But now that I looked closer, she didn't look angry. She looked . . . embarrassed?

"Hardly anyone saw you," I said. "Just Bruce and me and a couple of people behind the desk."

"That's good."

Okay, so that wasn't it either. I tried one more time. "The doctor says you'll be fine. It's nothing serious. Just hunger and, um . . ." I could feel myself getting red too. "You know, growing up."

Her hands clenched at the covers, and her hair fell farther forward to hide her face. I wasn't sure if I should keep talking or just leave her alone. But something made me think she didn't really want me to stop. She wasn't smiling and pretending nothing was wrong. I decided she wanted me to figure out what was bothering her but for some reason she couldn't just tell me.

"Are you thinking about Angela?"

Her head jerked back and her eyes met mine. "No," she whispered. "No, I wasn't thinking about her."

Her gaze slid into the distance and her brow furrowed. She was thinking about Angela now, and I cursed myself for bringing her up. Our little sister had died of cancer two years earlier, and Mom had certainly been thinking about her after Tania collapsed. Mom never stopped thinking about her.

I said, "Look, this is nothing like that. I'm sorry I mentioned it."

She shook her head. "It's all right, Jon. I'm not worried about dying."

I slumped back in my chair. "Well, what are you worried about? I want to help, but—"

Tania stared at me, her head tipped a little to one side. I could almost see the thinking going on behind the big blue eyes, but I didn't know *what* she was thinking. Her staring like that was worse than when she hid her face. I wanted to look away, but forced myself to meet her gaze. I hoped I looked kind and supportive.

Just when I thought I couldn't stand it anymore, she said, "You don't believe in ghosts, right?"

The tension broke and I laughed. "Of course not!"

She kept staring, her face serious and intent. "But all this stuff that Bruce does for his TV show, investigating psychic phenomenon and testing it . . ."

"That doesn't mean anything." Why was she bringing this up now? "We already talked about this with Dad, when we watched Bruce's show. Dad pointed out how Bruce never actually proved anything, even with all his gadgets. Mostly he just listens to people tell stories about seeing ghosts, and asks all those questions like, 'Could the ghost of Sir Wellington-Smith still be walking the halls of Broadmoor Manor?'"

I frowned at her, trying to figure out what this was all about. "Bruce is okay, but he's not a scientist. You can like him, but you don't have to believe him. And Mom—well, you know why Mom wants to believe in spirits. But that doesn't mean you have to believe in them."

That was one of the hard things from the last

few years. When Angela got sick, Dad consulted every medical specialist he could find. At first that was enough for Mom, too. But when Angela didn't get better, Mom started trying anything—prayer circles, faith healers, sending money to televangelists, probably voodoo rituals, for all I knew. That was what drove Mom and Dad apart, even more than the stress over Angela's death.

Tania looked down and then back up with that same urgent gaze. Her lips parted like she was going to speak, but nothing came out.

I said, "Come on, don't tell me you're starting to believe that nonsense."

"Oh, no. I've never believed in ghosts." She took a quick breath and let it out. "The only problem is, I just saw one."

CHAPTER
3

What could I say to that? I stared at Tania, trying to decide if she were joking or playing a trick on me. Her whole body looked tense, her face white, her eyes wide and pleading. My half smile faded.

"I saw a woman in a long, fancy dress standing at the top of the stairs."

I frowned. "I didn't see anyone on the stairs." Maybe it was just a shadow or a trick of the light.

"She appeared all of a sudden—I mean, I didn't think anyone was there, and then I saw her. I figured she must have just come around the corner." Now that she'd started talking, the words rushed out. "She looked awful. Like she just had the worst news in the world." Tania bit her lip and looked down. She whispered, "Like Mom, when Angela died."

I swallowed hard and cleared my throat, but I

still sounded hoarse when I spoke. "And then what happened?"

"She looked right at me. She started coming down the stairs. And that's when I realized I could see through her. I could still see the steps behind her as she came down. She was staring at me the whole time. When she was just a few feet away, she reached out for me. And then I guess I fainted."

We sat in silence for a long time. I could feel Tania's gaze still on my face, begging me to believe her, but I couldn't look at her.

Thoughts stormed in my mind. I wasn't sure what this story meant, but I knew it couldn't be good. I glanced at Tania's face and in that split second any last hope I had that she was joking faded. She believed she had seen a ghost. But I had been right beside her, and I hadn't seen a woman anywhere near the stairs.

Could Tania be going crazy?

I guess my thoughts showed on my face, because she looked down as pink crept up her cheeks. She sat perfectly still, her hands clenched in her lap, but I thought she was about to cry.

I sighed. Whatever had happened to Tania, whatever she had seen, something had scared her. We could figure out the rest later.

I got out of the chair and sat on the edge of the bed.

I wondered about hugging her, but that seemed awkward. So I just said, "I don't understand what happened. But I'll try to help."

She looked up. Tears shone in her eyes and her lips trembled, but she was sort of smiling, too. She threw her arms around me and I patted her shoulder. I didn't usually like her hugging me, but this time I was pretty sure I'd done the right thing.

She sat back, wiped the tears from her face, and gave me a real smile. "I was afraid you wouldn't believe me! I thought no one would."

I wasn't sure what I believed, but this was no time to mention that. Instead I said, "Bruce would believe you. Mom, too."

The smile vanished. She was silent.

A new idea came into my head. Had she made up this story to get their attention? Was she trying to get on Bruce's *Haunted* TV show? Maybe she was just a really good actress. Maybe she was testing her act on me, before trying it on Bruce.

She said, "You won't tell them?"

"What? Why not?"

She threw herself back against the pillows and hugged her knees to her chest. "Think about it! What would they do if I told them I'd seen a ghost?"

I frowned. "Well . . . they probably would believe

13

you. Bruce would be ecstatic and probably interview you for the TV show. And do tests and things . . ."

"Right. I don't want to be on TV. Just think about going back to school after that."

"You'd be famous."

"A famous nut! How would you like to be 'The Girl Who Sees Ghosts'?"

I grinned. "Well, I wouldn't want to be 'the girl' for starters." She didn't smile. I sighed and admitted, "A lot of kids would make fun of you."

"And Dad?"

I thought about that. "He'd probably think you were making it up to get Mom's and Bruce's attention." My face felt hot, since that was exactly what I had thought.

We didn't say anything for a while. And then Tania whispered, "And Mom?"

I stared at her as it hit me. I said slowly, "She'd want you to contact Angela." That was why Mom had gotten interested in ghost sightings in the first place. That was how she'd met Bruce. If Tania was making this up, this was more complicated than I could figure out. She didn't have enough to gain.

"And I can't!" Tania said. "I don't know if it will ever happen again. I hope it doesn't. Just because I see some ghosts doesn't mean I can control it."

"Wait a minute—some ghosts? You mean this isn't the first time?"

She gave me a guilty sideways look. "Well . . . this is the first time I've been sure."

I covered my face with my hands and groaned.

"I thought it was my imagination!"

I leaned back and sighed. "How long has this been going on?"

"A couple of months, I guess. Like I thought I saw Booger. Only it was just a glimpse, and kind of faint, like he wasn't really there. I figured I was just missing him."

Booger was our dog, who was hit by a car a few months earlier. Yes, I had named him, but I was only five at the time. "So you saw a ghost dog?"

"I don't know! It was just one of those things, I hardly noticed at the time. Then it happened again. Three times altogether, in about a week. But after that, it stopped. I thought it was some kind of grieving thing. Like after Angela died and sometimes I'd forget she was dead, and think I heard her crying in her room, but when I went there, it was Mom crying."

"But you never saw Angela?"

"No. I guess I'm glad for that. At least I think so." She shook her head. "I don't even know what to think or feel anymore."

This was getting stranger and stranger. I pretended I was Dad, the scientist, asking rational questions. "Anything else?"

"We drove past the graveyard once, and I saw this white blur by one of the graves. I told myself it was, you know, mist, or a trick of the light."

"Maybe it was."

"Maybe, that time. But not this time. This time I saw her just as clearly as I see you."

"But you said you could see through her."

"I could still see her clearly." Tania sighed. "It's hard to explain. But I could see her face, her expression. Her dress had big sleeves, and she was wearing gloves. I could even see the texture of the fabric. She was faded, kind of washed out, but not entirely white. I could tell she'd had brown hair, and her dress was maybe yellow or tan. It was long and fancy like a wedding dress, with a train that dragged behind, but it wasn't white."

"Yeah, that's some trick of the light," I admitted. "Okay. What do you want to do?"

She hugged her knees tighter and rested her chin on them. "I don't know."

I tried to think. We couldn't tell Mom, or Dad, or anyone. This had to be between just us, at least until something else happened and I knew more about what was going on. But Tania was scared. And maybe she was even going crazy. I didn't know what to do. I tried to think of anything that might help. "Let's call room service."

CHAPTER 4

We got grilled cheese sandwiches and tomato soup, which sounds boring, but it wasn't. The sandwiches had lots of cheddar cheese on some sort of fancy bread with seeds in it, and the soup had chunks of tomato and basil leaves floating in it. It was good, but there wasn't enough of it, even though I finished half of Tania's sandwich. (I know she was supposed to eat a lot, but she swore she'd had enough. I couldn't *force* her to eat.) I tried to talk about nice, dull things, although it was hard to find a safe topic, when I couldn't bring up our parents, the TV show, the hotel, or why we were there.

Besides, my brain was racing. I came up with four possibilities. One, Tania was going crazy. In that case, she needed real help, and I should tell someone what she'd said.

Two, Tania was playing a joke on me. I'd have to admire her if she pulled off that kind of prank, but it didn't seem her style. And if I told anyone else that she'd convinced me she'd seen a ghost, I'd look like an even bigger fool when the truth came out.

Three, she'd made a mistake. There was some logical explanation, and we just had to find it. But we'd both look like fools if we told anyone else now.

And four, ghosts were real. It was an exciting thought, but I couldn't make myself believe it. Since when was the world that interesting? But if ghosts were real, we didn't want to tell anyone that Tania could see them. Both for the reasons she'd mentioned, and because we could have a lot more fun on our own.

I have to admit, part of me was hoping for option four. Two and three would be all right, and they'd help to pass the time for a few hours, until I found out the truth. Of the choices, number one would be the worst. That was scary, and not something I could handle alone. But since three of the four options involved not telling anyone else, and that was what Tania wanted, I'd stick with that.

When we finished, I pushed the cart with the dirty dishes into the hallway. I turned back to the room and saw Tania standing and gazing at me expectantly. "What do we do now?" she asked. "How do we find out what happened?"

It figures. She's the one who sees a ghost, and I have to decide what to do about it. I walked to the window and gazed out over the grassy lawn to give myself time to think. This wasn't just going to go away. Tania might hope it never happened again, but she would always wonder what she had really seen, and worry about the next time. And I would always wonder if my little sister was loony. Somehow we had to find out the truth.

I turned back to her. "I guess we should investigate. We can go back to the stairs. Maybe you just made a mistake, and we'll figure out what it was."

She hunched her shoulders and wrinkled her nose. "Or maybe I'll see her again."

"Right. That will tell us something too." I smiled and tried to keep my voice casual, as if we were just planning a tour of the city. "And then we can ask about the history of the place. Previous ghost sightings, and so forth. Nobody will be surprised, since we're with the TV show."

Tania smiled. "All right." Her cheeks had color again. She almost looked excited, now that we had a plan. Or maybe she just assumed that I would make everything all right. Great.

I made sure I had the card key, then pulled the door shut behind us. "Which way do you want to go? To the top of the big staircase on this floor, or would you rather go down the elevator and hit the staircase from the bottom?"

Tania thought for a moment. She didn't sound too confident when she said, "I guess we should take the elevator and come at the stairs from the bottom. That will be most like what we did before."

"Sounds good," I said lightly. I thought it took some courage to make that choice, but I didn't say anything about that, because I didn't want to point out how bad it could be. Even if she didn't see anything this time, she'd be scared until we got there.

We went to the end of the hall and rode the elevator down in silence. Tania looked pale, and I hoped she wouldn't faint again. I'd get in big trouble if that happened.

We stepped out of the elevator onto the first floor. We could see down a wide hall to the reception area at the end, but the staircase was out of sight. Tania's hand crept into mine. I jumped a bit. I couldn't remember the last time she'd taken my hand. Probably years ago, when I was supposed to help her across the street. I'd been embarrassed back then to be seen holding hands with my little sister. But I reminded myself that none of my friends could see me, and I gave her hand a squeeze.

I just hoped Maggie wouldn't see us. I didn't want her to think I was a little kid. On the other hand, maybe she was old enough to think it sweet that I looked after my sister.

Tania took tiny steps down the corridor, pressed against my side. I felt like I was tripping over her feet, but I had to match her pace. The bottom step of the staircase came into view at the right side of the reception hall. Tania gripped my hand so hard, my fingers started to go numb. My heart beat faster. Of course we wouldn't see anything—there wouldn't be anything to see. But my heart hammered anyway, saying, *What if, what if?*

I could hear voices faintly, though I couldn't see anyone yet. Someone would be behind the long reception counter, but I hoped no one was checking in just then.

"There are people out there," I whispered. "We have to act normal."

Tania nodded. She let go of my hand and edged about three inches away.

I said, "If you feel like you're going to faint, just grab my arm. I'll try to haul you back over here before anyone notices."

More stairs came into view on the right. The second, third, fourth step. I realized I was holding my breath, and I let it out.

We moved closer. We could now see the counter, with two clerks behind it.

We stepped out of the corridor into the lobby.

For a second my vision blurred as I looked up at a brilliant, glowing light at the top of the stairs.

I blinked, and everything came into focus. At the top of the stairs, my stepfather stood in the glare of a spotlight, a few feet away from a camera. I took a step backward and tugged at Tania's arm. No one had seen us yet, and we could still escape.

She didn't back up. She swayed.

I took a quick step forward and put my arm around her so she wouldn't fall. I looked down into her face. I'd never seen anyone so white. White as death. Or white as a ghost.

"Tania," I hissed. I gave her a shake. She took a quick breath and dragged her eyes away from the staircase and to my face. The look in them made my stomach flip.

CHAPTER
5

I glanced up the stairs, but for me they were empty except for Bruce and the camera crew at the top.

"She's there," Tania whispered.

I stared at the staircase. "What's she doing?"

"She's coming down the stairs. She's staring straight at me."

I stared until my eyes stung and I had to blink. I shook my head. There was no ghost. I grinned down at Tania. "It's a joke, right? Okay, you got me."

She looked at me with her eyes blazing. Then her face crumpled and her chin started to tremble. "Oh, why can't you see her too?"

I didn't know what to say. Fortunately, Bruce's voice called out, "Kids!"

I stepped away from Tania. She stood straight, hands clenched at her side, and looked up toward Bruce. He jogged down the stairs toward us, with a big grin, like he was ready for the camera to start rolling again.

"I'm glad to see you up!" He peered at Tania. "You must be feeling better." She had color in her cheeks now, feverish red spots against her white skin. I thought she looked worse than before, but maybe Bruce was so used to TV makeup that he couldn't tell. His own face was powdered, with black eyeliner around his eyes.

"Did you want to see what we're doing?" Bruce dropped his arm around Tania's shoulders and pulled her toward the staircase. She shot a pleading look back at me. I wasn't sure what to do. I wanted to get out of there, but Bruce really wanted us to be interested in his show. And Mom would be hurt if she thought we were rude.

I trailed after them up the stairs. Bruce stopped at the landing and waved his arm. "This is where the ghost has been spotted—this very place!"

Tania and I exchanged glances. I asked, "What kind of ghost?"

Bruce said in a low, dramatic voice, "A bride who died on her wedding day."

Tania raised her eyebrows and gave me a triumphant little smile. I ignored her, because Bruce was watching me. He added, "We're going to call her either the Ghost Bride or the Lady in White."

Tania had said the dress wasn't really white, but I could hardly point that out to Bruce. I said, "Lady in White? Isn't that a bit, you know, cliché?"

Bruce grinned. "I know you're a skeptic, Jon. That's good. You shouldn't believe everything you're told. I sure don't, and I've seen a lot of strange things! I don't say that there *is* such a ghost, but people have reported seeing her many times over the last century."

"And you think you'll find her now? Capture her on film, or whatever?"

"If only I could! Ghosts are notoriously hard to get on film. Lots of people have thought they had a picture of a ghost only to develop the film and find out it got fogged or damaged somehow." Bruce kept smiling. His perfect white teeth and floppy, highlighted hair were really starting to irritate me.

He said, "We'll film the hotel, and interviews with hotel staff who have seen the ghost. I'll use my gadgets to see if I can get readings of any strange forces. You wouldn't believe the electromagnetic field readings here. And we'll have somebody dress up as the ghost to re-create the sightings."

I opened my mouth, but before I could speak, he went on. "Oh, don't worry! We're not faking a sighting. We'll make it clear that this is just an actress. But it makes the show more dramatic."

"Sure, I can see that." I glanced at Tania, who was watching me expectantly. She wasn't going to be much help investigating her ghost. I tried to think what to ask next. "So this ghost, who is she? What's her story?"

Bruce smiled that toothpaste-ad grin. "That's what we're here to find out. Watch the filming!"

I bit back three or four things I really wanted to say, and finally muttered, "So can we watch the filming and everything?"

"Absolutely! Just make sure you keep quiet and stay out of the camera's line of sight. And let me know if you see any ghosts!"

Tania jumped and flushed guiltily. She looked over her shoulder, at nothing I could see, and edged closer to me. Pretty funny that Bruce couldn't see a ghost when he wanted to, and that Tania could see it even though she didn't want to. I guess that's what they call irony.

"We'll let you know." I chuckled, as if the idea was ridiculous. "So, um, what are you up to now?"

"We're going to do some interviews in a few minutes. We have to set up the lighting, and make sure all the equipment is working." He gestured toward an open black case with a bunch of gadgets stuck in it.

"What does that stuff actually do?"

"Let me show you." Bruce pulled me toward the case. I looked back at Tania. She gestured and made faces at me. I mouthed, shhh! What did she want me to do, anyway?

"You should appreciate this equipment, with your interest in science," Bruce said.

Tania tugged on my arm. "What?" I hissed.

She stretched up to whisper in my ear. "The ghost is right here. She's watching us!"

CHAPTER
6

I got a little shiver from that. I had to look over my shoulder, even though I knew I wouldn't see anything. Before I could think what to do or say, Bruce was talking.

"We think that ghosts cause changes in energy fields, and these tools can detect that. In the early days of ghost hunting, people used ordinary compasses. The compass needle would spin if a ghost was present. That looked impressive, but I think these other tools are more scientific. Most of them were designed to detect energy leaks in buildings, things like that. The fact that they may detect ghosts is a happy accident."

I didn't know what do about the ghost, or Tania, so I tried to pay attention to Bruce. If ghosts were real, learning this stuff might help.

He pulled out a small black plastic thing. "This is an electromagnetic field meter. If the reading jumps way up or down, that might mean you have a ghost."

"Wait a minute," I said. "If the reading goes up *or* down? Shouldn't it be one or the other?"

"Well, we think spirits are made of energy, and so may give off energy. But some spirits seem to drain energy from the area, maybe using it to manifest. We don't really understand it all that well."

"Obviously," I muttered.

"But anything unusual may be significant. Of course, first we have to make sure that it's not something artificial in the house, like an appliance, an electrical outlet, or a power line in the wall."

"How can you ever be really sure of that?"

Bruce grinned. "I've done investigations in cemeteries, where there wasn't any power! In places like this, you have to study the building plans. You also look for corroboration. For example, if you feel a cold spot, and the camera picks up bright floating spheres, and you also have a spike on your EMF reader, that's good evidence."

Or a lot of random coincidences. Bruce might call it science, but that didn't make it fact. They had a theory that ghosts were made of energy, so they used energy detection devices to try to find ghosts. Maybe they really were finding energy, but that didn't mean they were detecting ghosts. What if they were wrong about what ghosts were made of? It all seemed pretty sketchy to me.

"Here, try it," Bruce said. He put the gadget in my hand. "Wrap your hand around the bottom, with your fingers on the side. Don't cover the end of the meter— that's where the sensors are. Bend your elbow like this." He pulled and prodded me until my arm was partly extended, the meter held level to the ground. "Now move the meter from side to side."

"So this is supposed to tell me if a ghost is here?"

Tania looked to her right and bit her lip, so I aimed the gadget that way. The meter's needle started bobbing around.

"Gently!" Bruce said. "If you move it too quickly, or up and down, you can get false readings. It takes a delicate touch."

"Uh-huh. Here, Tania, you try it." I figured she knew where the ghost was, so we could get evidence of whether this thing really worked.

But Tania shook her head. "Oh no, no thanks."

I kept holding out the gadget. "Come on, it's easy, give it a try."

She wrinkled her nose and shook her head.

"Maybe she'd rather try the Geiger counter," Bruce said. "Geiger counters can detect changes in radiation. Every house has some background radiation, but spikes or dips might indicate a spirit."

He turned back toward the box. Tania edged closer to me and whispered, "I can't point those things at her. It seems rude!"

Bruce held out another gadget, but Tania shook her head. I chuckled. "Tania's not so crazy about technology." She scowled at me. Well, what was I supposed to say if she was going to act weird?

Bruce grinned. "She leaves the science to you, huh? Too bad—we use lots of these gadgets. Infrared motion detectors, relative humidity gauges, ion particle counters, and of course fancy thermometers. Ghosts are also associated with cold spots. So you see, Jon, I do use a lot of science in my research!"

Fortunately, I didn't have to answer, because Tania broke in. "So what good does it all do? Say you do prove there's a ghost here—then what?"

"Then we've learned a little more about the world!"

"But what about the ghost?" she asked. "What do you do about it?" When Bruce just frowned, looking puzzled, she elaborated. "This woman who died here, who's still here as a ghost. That's sad. Can't you help her somehow?"

Bruce put his arm around Tania. "Honey, if we could find a way to talk to the ghosts, that would be fabulous. Helping them is a great idea, very sweet. But right now, we're just trying to prove that ghosts exist. Communicating with them, well, that's a great dream for the future, but we just don't know how to do it right now."

Tania nodded, but she was frowning, staring into the distance. You could see she was still thinking hard.

One of the staff members piped up. "Ready for the interviews."

"Well, you're busy, so we ought to go," I said. "Thanks for showing us all that."

"All right. See you kids later." He gave Tania's shoulder a pat. "Glad you're feeling better!" He jogged toward the camera people, who were mumbling over a clipboard full of papers.

I glanced at Tania and jerked my head toward the stairs. She followed me down. Without speaking, we crossed the lobby and went out the main doors. As we left, Tania glanced back. Whatever she saw made her move faster.

CHAPTER

7

I blinked in the afternoon sunshine and gazed out over smooth green lawns. Everything looked happy and peaceful. I took a few steps away from the hotel and looked back at it. The gray stone looked cold, even in the sun. I shivered a little.

I glanced at Tania, hoping she hadn't noticed. It was stupid to get creeped out by this. I didn't believe in ghosts, and I hadn't seen anything to change my mind. There had to be another explanation.

Bruce's gadgets hadn't convinced me of anything. A lot of people don't understand the difference between a hypothesis and a theory. A hypothesis is basically a guess. Usually a good guess, based on what we know, but it has to be tested. In science, a theory is an accepted explanation based on all the best available data.

Like gravity—we know gravity exists because things don't just float away. The theory just takes all the known facts and puts them together to try to explain how gravity works. Maybe some of the details will change, as scientists get new information. But chances are, the basic theory will hold. Bruce's ideas about ghosts being energy sounded more like a guess, a hypothesis at best. Not a theory yet.

Tania said, "Now what?"

"What exactly did you see this time?"

"The same thing. A woman in a long dress. The Ghost Bride."

Now that I had time to think about it, I wasn't so impressed that Tania had seen the ghost that was supposed to be here. She could have heard about it ahead of time. Bruce and Mom might have talked about it. The hotel might even mention it in their brochures or on their website. So Tania could still be making it up.

But I had decided she had no reason to do that. But maybe she wasn't doing it on purpose. Maybe she had some subconscious reason, and thought she was seeing a ghost when she wasn't really. Thoughts tumbled around in my head and I couldn't sort them out.

Tania was watching me, waiting for me to figure out what to do. The only thing I could think of was to keep acting like there really was a ghost. "So what did she do?"

"She walked down the stairs, looking right at me, but then Bruce came down and she sort of dissolved."

"But you acted like you saw her again later."

"Yes, she appeared at the top of the stairs after we got up there."

"Wait a minute, when you say appeared—do you mean she walked up the stairs, or she, you know, *appeared*. Manifested, or whatever they call it."

"She appeared, kind of faded in. The opposite of when she dissolved. She just stood and watched us. She kept looking at me, like she knew I was the one who could see her."

"She didn't say anything?"

"No. When she came down the stairs, she opened her mouth like she was screaming or crying, but I didn't hear anything."

"I wonder if we could talk to her."

Tania said, "You mean I should try to speak to her, and see if she answers?"

I hadn't thought that far, but it made sense. "Yes, but we have to do it sometime when no one's around."

"There's probably always somebody at that counter."

I ran my fingers through my hair. Why did this have to be so complicated? "Maybe I can distract the clerks. Get them to go outside for a minute or something."

Tania wrinkled her nose and hunched her shoulders. "I don't want to talk to that ghost alone."

I sighed. We could try back late at night and hope they didn't have a clerk on duty. But that meant waiting all day, and that would drive Tania crazy—if she wasn't already. Besides, the TV show was only there for a couple of days, so we didn't have much time.

"All right," I said. "Let's go back in now. We can just stand near the bottom of the stairs and pretend that we're talking to each other and watching the filming."

Tania nodded. She looked down, then back up, and spoke softly. "Do you think she could be dangerous?"

I shrugged. I wasn't sure she was *anything*. But that got me wondering: Could a ghost do anything to you? Did it matter if you could see it or not?

I watched Tania as she stepped toward the door. Maybe we were going to find out.

CHAPTER

8

The camera crew filled the place now. Bruce stood at the top of the stairs with a lady in a hotel uniform. We stopped just inside the door.

"Do you see her?" I asked.

"Yes. She was watching Bruce and that lady, but now she's coming down the stairs." Tania took a deep breath and set her shoulders.

A man bustled over, scowling, and grabbed me by the arm. "You kids get back," he hissed. "They're filming."

"I know," I whispered. "That's our stepdad. He said we could watch."

The man's scowl deepened. He was about thirty, with dark spiky hair, and deep grooves alongside his mouth. I guess he scowled a lot. "Then keep quiet. Film is expensive, and you could ruin the take if you make noise."

I wanted to point out that he was the one making

all the noise, but instead I just nodded. I pulled my arm away, and Tania and I moved to the corner of the room, behind the end of the check-in desk.

I looked at Tania, raised my eyebrows, and mouthed the words, "What do you want to do now?"

Tania studied the scene for a minute, then stretched up to breathe the words in my ear. "Let's wait. The ghost is staying over there."

We turned our attention to Bruce's interview. The woman was about fifty, plump and plain, in a brown skirt and matching jacket. She had on makeup, too much of it, but I bet the TV people did that to her. She looked like normally she wouldn't bother.

Bruce had been grinning at the camera, introducing her, I guess. Now he turned toward her. "So tell me, Mary, when did you first see the ghost bride?"

"I was twelve years old," the lady said. She talked too fast and sounded short of breath, like she was nervous.

Bruce had an interested, sympathetic look. "Tell me about it."

"I'd been to the hotel several times before, as a child. My family used to come sometimes to eat in the restaurant. I'd heard stories, of course, but this was the first time I actually saw her."

"And what did you see?" Bruce asked, in his deep, TV announcer voice.

The woman took a deep breath. "We came through those doors." She pointed, even though the camera wouldn't be able to see the doors. "My father greeted someone he knew, and they started talking. I just stood there at the bottom of the stairs. Then I looked up and saw this woman coming down the stairs. She was wearing an old-fashioned dress. I mean, old-fashioned for even back then, and this was forty years ago."

"A wedding dress," Bruce said.

The woman's forehead scrunched up. "Well, I don't know. It didn't look like wedding dresses today, or even back then. It had long, loose sleeves, and a skirt that dragged behind her. It might have been a wedding dress. It was certainly fancy."

"And then what happened?" Bruce asked.

"Well, she started coming down the stairs, and at first I was just interested because she had on this fancy dress, and it wasn't what anyone wore back then. The dress was so pretty, so of course I was interested in her."

Bruce kept his grin, but his voice sounded a little impatient as he said, "And what did the ghost do?"

"Well, she started down the stairs, and I just thought, there must be a costume party or a fancy dress ball, or something like that. And I just stood and watched her. But there was something funny about her, like she was kind of blurry. I thought maybe the light was bad, or my eyes weren't working right. I needed glasses, you see, and I'd only had them a little while, so I wasn't quite used to them."

"And then?"

Tania stretched up to whisper again. "The ghost is going back up the stairs toward them. I think she understands what that woman said. Maybe that means she can communicate!"

I could barely hear Tania with her mouth two inches from my ear, but the scowling man turned to glare at us again.

The woman frowned as she went on with her story. "She came farther down the stairs, and I thought I could see through her. And I looked at her face, and she looked so sad, so miserable. I felt really bad for her, because, you know, I was twelve years old, and I thought that anyone who dressed like that, who must be going to a fancy party, or getting married or something, well, they should be happy. But she didn't look happy. She looked like she'd been crying."

Tania gripped my arm. "That's it! That's exactly what it was like! That woman saw her too."

I nodded, but didn't say anything, because the mean guy started walking toward us with his scowl. I kept my gaze on the interview. The jerk stopped on the other side of the check-in desk and made gestures with his hands. I stared over him, pretending not to see.

"I see," Bruce said. "Did she come all the way down the stairs?"

"Yes, she got to the bottom. And she looked at me like she knew I could see her."

"And then what?"

"Then my daddy finished his conversation, and he came over and took my arm, and led me into dinner. I didn't want to go, but I didn't want to tell him what I had seen, so I went with him."

Bruce nodded, looking serious. "And did you ever see the Ghost Bride again?"

I glanced at Tania, whose eyes were fixed on the woman's face.

"Yes, four or five times. After that first time, of course I was curious. So I snuck back to the hotel a few more times. We only went as a family on special occasions, and then of course I didn't have much freedom."

"And you saw her again?"

"Yes. It was always just the same. I wanted to talk to her, because she looked so sad, but I was afraid, too."

"The Ghost Bride frightened you?"

"Oh no, I wasn't afraid of her. She just looked so unhappy. But I was afraid people would think I was crazy if I told them I was seeing a ghost and trying to talk to her. There were always people around."

The front door rattled—it looked like maybe someone was trying to come in—so the mean guy hustled off to deal with that emergency.

"So you saw the Ghost Bride several times," Bruce said.

"And then I stopped seeing her. We came for my fourteenth birthday—I'd asked for that. But I didn't see her that time, or ever again. I never imagined back then that I would be working at the hotel someday, and even to this day I sometimes hope that I'll see her. Sometimes I think I feel her. I just get the sense that she's still there, but I haven't seen her in almost forty years." She looked genuinely sad, as if she missed her old friend, the unhappy ghost. "Sometimes, when I'm coming up the stairs, I'll whisper a little hello, just in case she can hear me."

Tania whispered, "The ghost is right next to her, listening. She reached out her hand, like she's going to touch her."

The woman shuddered, like she'd gotten a sudden chill. She tugged her jacket a little closer.

Bruce turned to the camera. "Well, that's the story from Mary Watson, the hotel's supervising housekeeper, who sighted the ghost several times, back when she was just a girl, and believes she can still feel the ghost today." Bruce kept smiling for a few seconds, then said, "All right, cut."

The camera operator did something to the camera, then stepped back and stretched. Bruce turned his TV-star grin to Mrs. Watson and shook her hand. Then she went off somewhere down the hallway.

I looked at Tania. "What do you think?"

She beamed up at me. "I can't believe it! She saw just what I saw. I'm so glad I'm not the only one."

"Yeah, and she saw it all years ago."

"When she was about my age," Tania said, frowning. "I wonder what that means."

Bruce called out, "All right, let's start the next interview."

"Do you want to keep watching?" I asked Tania.

"Oh, yes! It feels good to hear about other people who have seen her. It makes me feel like I'm not crazy after all."

Made sense. Until I saw the next interview subject. I wasn't sure that I would want to be associated with *her* in any way.

CHAPTER
9

She was a tall, thin woman, with fiery red hair, obviously dyed. She was draped in all this wispy, colorful cloth, like she couldn't find any real clothes and had to get dressed in scarves that morning. She had on pale face makeup, with red lips and big dark eyes, and somehow I didn't think that was just the TV people's work. She looked like she should be holding a crystal ball, or inviting you to get your fortune told over the phone on a late-night commercial.

It took a few minutes for everyone to settle into place. Then Bruce did his introduction. The woman called herself Madame Natasha, and said she was a psychic who lived in Denver. She spoke in a theatrical voice that swooped up and down and around. "When I first heard of the Ghost Bride, of course I wanted to meet her. I have always been interested in manifestations from the beyond. I'm a sensitive, in tune with the spiritual world. I often pick up vibrations of the Other, and frequently see or feel ghostly manifestations."

"I see." Bruce nodded seriously. "So you came to the hotel specifically to look for the Ghost Bride?"

"Yes indeed. How could I pass up the opportunity to meet such an intriguing person?"

"And what happened?"

"As soon as I entered the door, I felt at once that this was a place of ghostly tragedy. The air simply thrilled with emotion."

"And you saw the ghost?"

"Yes, I saw her at once. She stood at the top of the stairs, a tall, beautiful woman, in a long, white wedding gown, with a lace veil pulled back from her face, revealing a tumble of golden curls. She was beaming happily, the perfect picture of a young woman on her wedding day."

Tania nudged me and muttered, "That's not right at all!"

"She moved down the stairs gracefully," the woman went on, "an image of youth and beauty. And then, when she was halfway down—" The psychic paused dramatically.

"Yes?" Bruce said in a voice deep with emotion.

The psychic turned her head and put a hand to her brow. "It is hard even to speak of it. Suddenly she stopped. Her face changed. She raised her hands and cried out with anguish, 'My husband! Where is my husband who has abandoned me!'"

Tania was staring. "She heard the ghost speak?"

The mean guy took a couple of steps toward us, so I elbowed Tania to be quiet.

The psychic said, "Then she buried her face in her hands, weeping. I went forward. I wanted to reach out, to comfort her. I hoped that with my skills, I might be able to offer some small moment of peace to this tragic creature. But she dissolved in front of my eyes. A poor, abandoned bride, waiting for her lover for eternity."

"And did you ever see her again?" Bruce asked.

"I am hoping that I shall see her this week," the psychic said. "That is why I am staying at the hotel. I would like to speak to the Ghost Bride, to hear her story."

"Well, we shall certainly hope that you manage to do so," Bruce said. "We would like to film your attempts."

Madame Natasha's smile flashed so quickly, I wasn't sure I'd really seen it. Then she was looking serious again. "Well, I must have the right conditions to reach the ghost. But if the filming doesn't interfere, I'd be delighted to aid in the advancement of knowledge."

I made sure the mean guy wasn't watching us, then whispered to Tania, "What does the ghost think of her?"

Tania scrunched up her face. "She listened at first. She even stood right in front of that Madame whatever. Then she seemed to lose interest and move away."

Bruce and the psychic exchanged a few more words. Then he turned to the camera, grinning like a maniac. "We've just heard Madame Natasha's story, and a dramatic story it is, of one ordinary woman using her gifts to reach into the beyond."

Somehow I didn't think Madame Natasha was ordinary, or that she would want to be described that way. She stood there, gazing into the distance with this dreamy look, like you were supposed to believe she was all spiritual or something. They stopped the camera and Bruce shook the woman's hand vigorously.

"So what did you think of that?" I muttered to Tania.

Her nose wrinkled. "I think she's lying. The other woman was telling the truth, but this woman, she just wants to get on TV. She probably only came to look for the ghost because she heard about the show filming here. Then she made up something so Bruce would interview her."

"Could be," I said, "but Bruce seems to like her."

Madame Natasha went off along the second-floor hallway. Bruce jogged down the stairs and went into conference with Mom and some of the camera people. We edged closer to listen.

"Now *that* was a fantastic interview," Bruce said. "We'll use that one. It will be great for the first segment. We can do a follow-up, when she tries to contact the ghost. She said she'd wait until tomorrow."

"What about the other lady?" someone asked. "The housekeeper."

Bruce shook his head. "Waste of film. Boring story, unphotogenic subject."

"She seemed nice enough," Mom protested.

"Oh, nice, sure," Bruce said. "But who really wants to hear about her little sighting forty years ago? Besides, she babbled. But Madame Natasha!" Bruce stroked his chin thoughtfully. "There's a woman with presence. I wonder if we could get her to come to some of our other locations, to see if she could spot the ghosts there."

Mom frowned. She obviously disapproved, but I didn't know if she thought Madame Natasha was a fraud, or if she was afraid that Bruce had the hots for the psychic. That was a disgusting thought.

I nudged Tania. "Let's get out of here."

Tania glanced toward the stairs. "Just a minute. Everyone's busy, so I want to try to talk to her."

I followed her nervously. The TV crew had gathered by the check-in counter, around the side of the staircase. They were deep in conversation, but they could still see us. I was already afraid that Mom would be mad I had let Tania out of bed. I didn't need her fainting again.

Tania stood at the bottom of the stairs and gazed up. She had this intent look on her face. I found myself staring at the stairs as well. I saw a bit of movement at the top. Madame Natasha poked her head around the corner and looked down at the TV crew. Then she saw me watching her and ducked back.

I couldn't see anything else on the stairs, so I turned to watch Tania instead.

Her eyes got wider, and she drew her body back without actually moving her feet. "She's staring at me," she whispered.

My heart was pounding again. It was the creepiest thing, seeing Tania react that way to something I couldn't see. "Talk to her," I said.

Tania's voice shook. "Hello? Who are you? What do you want?"

Suddenly Tania gasped and kind of shuddered. I grabbed her arm. It was like grabbing a block of ice.

"What happened?" I hissed.

Tania's mouth moved, but no words came out. Her eyes stared straight ahead.

CHAPTER
10

I grabbed Tania's arm and dragged her through the door, out into the sunshine.

I pulled her away from the door, out of sight of anyone inside. I glanced around. No one was close enough to pay attention to us. I rubbed Tania's arms, trying to get some heat into her. She started shivering violently. She blinked fast and took big gasping breaths.

"You're okay," I said. "It's all right now."

But it wasn't all right. That couldn't have been faked. You can't just make yourself suddenly ice cold.

Tania pushed my hands away. "I'm fine." She sank down to the grass. She hugged her knees. I sat next to her, making sure my shadow wasn't blocking any of the sun on her.

I refused to believe my sister was crazy or sick. I just couldn't handle that. Life was too complicated already. And even the thought of having something awful happen to Tania made me feel like an elephant was sitting on my chest. I couldn't lose another sister.

I had to believe in her, believe she was healthy and sane. So that meant we had a ghost. I had a sister who could see a ghost.

All right, fine. But I didn't have to get weird about it. My father was an engineer. He said a few scientists change their results, or only report part of them, when their experiments show something different from what they believe. That was bad science. Good scientists observe and record the facts, without bias. Then they try to figure out what it all means. I had to be a good scientist here. I had to use logic.

How do you use logic with a ghost?

I took a deep breath. I had to figure this out. "Can you tell me what happened?"

"She came down the stairs like before. It's like she knows I can see her and most people can't. She's not paying any attention to you."

Oh, darn. I was so insulted.

"When she got close, she reached out her hand. And she touched me." Tania gave one last violent shudder. "It was like falling through the ice into a lake. I've never been so cold in my life."

"That sounds pretty awful," I said. Actually, it sounded dangerous. But no one else had acted like the ghost was threatening. "Do you think the ghost was trying to hurt you?"

"No. I think she wants to tell me something, but she can't. Her mouth was moving, but I didn't hear any sounds."

"Do you think you could read her lips?" I couldn't believe I was asking that question about a ghost.

Tania frowned, then shook her head. "I don't think she was even saying actual words. It looked more like wailing. I don't think she knows how to communicate with real people anymore. But I could feel what she was feeling. And she's so unhappy! It's awful."

I had to smile. That's my sister, freaked out and frozen, and she still feels sorry for the ghost. "Well, maybe—"

The door opened behind us and I clamped my mouth shut. I swung around as Maggie stepped outside. I felt myself going red.

"There you two are. I have an hour free, so I thought we could get some ice cream." Maggie glanced out over the lawns, and she didn't smile. She looked bored.

My face got hotter. We didn't need a babysitter. Especially a bored one. "No thank you. We don't want to waste your valuable time."

She really looked at me for the first time. Suddenly she smiled, a real, honest smile. My breath caught in my chest and I found myself smiling back. "All right," she said. "Let me know if there is anything you want to do."

I just stared at Maggie, unable to think of anything to say.

Finally Tania said, "Could you tell us more about the Ghost Bride?"

Maggie switched her gaze to Tania and I could think again. Maggie said, "It hardly seems like the right time for ghost stories. Too much sunshine. But sure, I'll tell you what I know." She grinned. "How about we get that ice cream while we talk, though. I want some, anyway."

"Me too," Tania said.

A chance to learn about the ghost, spend time looking at Maggie, and eat ice cream too? I shrugged and grinned. "I guess I can be talked into it."

"Let's walk into town," Maggie said. "It's not far, and there's an ice-cream shop on the main drag."

"You've been here before?" I asked.

"I had to scout it out. They send me along ahead of time to make sure that the place is photogenic and that the people we need to interview will sound good on tape."

I said, "It must be interesting work."

"Oh, sure. I'm not changing the world, but I guess there are worse ways to spend my time."

I looked at her out of the corner of my eye as she talked about her job. I wondered how old she was. At least twenty, and maybe as old as twenty-five. Definitely grown up. It was silly to get all tongue-tied around her—but try telling that to my tongue. Well, at least she wasn't treating me like a little kid anymore.

Maggie asked Tania about school. They chattered as we walked into a town that looked like something out of a 1950s movie. Lots of shops that girls would call "cute," with flower boxes and fancy wooden trim. Everything looked newly painted. I saw a barbershop with an actual red-and-white pole, a Sweet Shoppe, and lots of little stores selling trinkets, antiques, or art. No fast-food restaurants in sight.

Tania said, "Oh!" and clapped her hands together. I followed her gaze to the ice-cream shop, which was just as cute as everything else. It had a big-eyed, smiling cow on the sign and curtains with little dancing cows in the windows. Inside, I ordered a double-scoop waffle cone, pistachio and Rocky Road. Maggie paid.

We sat at a small, round table by the window. Tania chatted happily, occasionally taking a tiny spoonful of her cup of cookie dough ice cream. She looked like a normal eleven-year-old girl, not someone who had just seen a ghost. I wondered again if she could be making up the whole thing. It just seemed too outrageous, especially when I had been there every time and hadn't seen a thing. She glanced at me, and I guess I was looking at her funny, because she stopped in the middle of a sentence. Pink spread up her cheeks and she looked down, letting her hair fall across her face. Maggie glanced between us.

I smiled and said quickly, "Your ice cream's melting, Tania." Tania started scooping up the melted pools from her cup. I grinned at Maggie. "That's why she's so thin. You have to remind her to eat."

"I'm sure she'll fill out nicely in the next couple of years," Maggie said. "She's going to be a beauty."

Tania peeked out from between her walls of hair and smiled shyly.

I scrabbled for something to say. "So, you were going to tell us about this Ghost Bride."

"Ah, yes. Her. What do you want to know?" Maggie licked ice cream from her cone and for a moment I completely forgot what we were talking about. I swallowed and forced my mind back to ghosts.

I guess I could have asked a lot of things, but what actually came out of my mouth was, "Do you really believe in this stuff?"

CHAPTER
11

Maggie frowned. My face got hot. I guess it was a pretty stupid question for someone who worked on *Haunted*.

Maggie looked at Tania and then back at me. "Look, I'll be honest with you, but . . . you won't tell Bruce, will you?"

Tania and I exchanged puzzled glances. Maggie grinned. "I guess I shouldn't ask you to keep secrets from your stepfather," she said. "All right, I'll be honest with you anyway. I don't believe in that . . . stuff. Ghosts and all. I've worked on this show for a year now, and I haven't seen anything to change my mind. But the work is interesting and fun, and I like Bruce."

"What would happen if he found out you don't believe?" Tania asked.

"Nothing, I guess. We don't have to believe in order to work on the show. It's not in our contract or anything. But Bruce is so enthusiastic . . . I just never told him I'm a skeptic. I try to go along with things and be as enthusiastic as he is."

"So why are you telling us?" I asked.

"I guess because you're young and, well—don't take offense—impressionable. At least kids are supposed to be. And if everyone around you is telling you this stuff is true, maybe you'll believe it without really figuring it out for yourselves." She chuckled. "I don't suppose this is what your mom had in mind when she asked me to look after you."

"You didn't want to." I didn't realize I was going to speak until the words were out.

"Yeah." Maggie shrugged. "I'm sorry. I didn't want to be a babysitter. But you two are okay—you're not as young as I thought. We can be friends, right?"

My heart raced and my palms were sweating. "Of course," I croaked. "That would be great."

Tania said something. I only caught her last words: "Right, Jon?"

"Huh? Oh yeah, sure."

They seemed to be waiting for me to say something else. "What about all those gadgets Bruce has? Do they do anything at all?"

Maggie grinned. "Sure. They flash lights and make beeping noises."

"Bruce said something about electric fields."

"Electromagnetic fields," Maggie corrected. "They're a combination of electric fields and magnetic fields. Some ghost hunters claim that if you get a reading, it means there's something there we can't see. But lots of things cause electromagnetic fields. It's like claiming that a change in temperature means there's a ghost. It could just be a draft."

"Isn't there any way to get real proof?" Tania asked.

Maggie finished her cone and leaned her elbows on the table. "It depends on what you call proof. Some people claim that blurry spots on a video are proof. The strangest thing for me is the Electronic Voice Phenomenon. That's when you hear voices on a tape recording that you didn't hear when the recording was made. I've been there for both the recording and the playback, and if someone altered the tape, I can't figure out how they did it. But I still don't call that proof. To me, the gadgets are just modern versions of the amulets."

"What amulets?" I asked.

"Bruce hasn't shown you those?" Maggie chuckled and shook her head. "He's collected all these so-called artifacts that are supposed to be used in exorcisms. He doesn't use them much on the TV show, because he wants to look scientific. But there are some wild items in there. Ask him sometime. He'll be happy to show you."

Tania and I exchanged glances. There had to be something useful here, though I wasn't sure what.

I leaned back in my chair and gave Maggie my best casual smile. "So, friend—what can we expect from this whole ghost thing? Who is this alleged ghost that you don't believe in? And what do we do about her?"

"You don't have to do a darn thing if you don't want to. You can stay in your room and watch TV all day, and let me do the work!"

I grinned. "Would we do that to a friend? Anyway, it's kind of interesting—how you put a TV show together, and all that."

"I guess it does seem glamorous, when you don't actually work in the business. No doubt you'll find it dull after you've done a couple of these. But I'm sure the camera operators and sound guy would be happy to show you what they do." She smiled at Tania. "You could have the makeup artist do your face sometime."

I could listen to Maggie talk about anything. But I had to get her talking about the ghost. "That technical stuff is cool, but what about the other part of the show? How do you put the story together? Take this place— what do you know about this ghost? What is she supposed to be?"

"Well, the story is that sometime back in the 1890s, this couple got married and went to the hotel for their honeymoon. They checked in, then the husband went out for some reason. He never came back. The Ghost Bride is still waiting for him."

"That's so sad!" Tania said. "No wonder—"

Maggie looked at her. "No wonder what?"

"Um, no wonder Bruce wants it for his TV show." Tania looked at me.

I jumped in. "That's right, Bruce said she died on her wedding day. I figured he was just being . . . um, you know."

"Melodramatic?" Maggie said. "Well, he was, a bit. She actually died a few days later. The story is that she went crazy, thinking her new husband had abandoned her. They found her one morning, dressed in her wedding gown, at the bottom of those big stairs."

"Wow." Brilliant comment, Jon.

"It's a great story," Maggie said. "I'm sure that's why the ghost tale came about. People saw or heard or felt something kind of weird, so they decided it had to be a ghost, and that woman's story is so dramatic. She's a natural to become a ghost."

"So you actually know who she is?" Tania asked. "You know her name?"

"No, that part of the story didn't come down clearly. I guess people didn't start claiming to see the ghost for a few years. Then they thought back about who might have become a 'Ghost Bride.' They remembered this story, and it seemed to fit, so they decided that's where the ghost came from."

"But you think the story about the couple is true?" Tania asked.

Maggie shrugged. "It might be. Tales like that usually come from somewhere. The story is dramatic and sad, so it probably got handed down, even though people weren't sure of the real names."

"Can't you check that kind of thing?" I asked. "They keep records of marriages and all that, right?" I was glad to make an intelligent comment.

Maggie smiled at me. "If you had a name, you could probably check for a record of a marriage. But without names, what are you looking for? Everyone who got married in the 1890s? How do you know which couple is the right one? So you see, it's the perfect ghost story. All rumor and gossip, nothing you can prove or disprove."

Something buzzed. "Uh-oh. That's my pager." Maggie stood and pulled her sweater up a few inches so she could see the pager. "Bruce wants me back at the hotel. You two stay here and finish your ice cream. Then look around town if you want. It's a cute little place, and impossible to get lost with only one main street." She smiled and waved as she headed for the door.

I stared after her and then looked at Tania. She

wrinkled her nose at me and said, "Well, it's a start. That poor woman."

"Yeah. Abandoned on her wedding day. Harsh."

"So what are we going to do about it?" Tania asked.

I shrugged. "Why do we have to do anything? So you saw a ghost. A real ghost of a real person. Now we know who she was. You can just avoid her for the next couple of days. Stay away from the stairs."

"But I can't!"

"Sure you can. Just use the elevator. There's probably even another entrance."

Tania rolled her eyes. "I don't mean that. I mean I can't just forget this happened. What if it happens again? If we travel with the show, we could run into all kinds of ghosts."

Yikes. I hadn't thought of that.

"Anyway, that's not all," Tania said. "She needs our help."

"Help!" A couple of people turned to look at me, and I lowered my voice. "How do we help a ghost? Get a ghost psychiatrist to counsel her through her grief? Or maybe a priest—hey, that's not such a bad idea. We could do an exorcism."

"No, we can't—"

"You're right: How could we get a priest to do it without telling what you'd seen? Maybe we could suggest it to Bruce—no, he likes ghosts. He wouldn't want to get rid of it. And the hotel likes it for tourists. A real fake English castle with a real ghost."

"It's not that!" Tania said. "I want to do something for her. She's so unhappy, and she must have been like this for over a hundred years. I want to help."

Dad always said Tania was softhearted. More like softheaded, if you asked me. "But what can we possibly do that would help her?"

"We can find out what happened to her husband."

I sighed. I guess this wasn't just going to go away. "Okay, so let's say we figure out what happened to her husband. Then what? How do we tell the ghost?"

Tania scowled. "I'll find a way."

That gave me a chill, almost worse than anything so far. After seeing what the ghost's touch did to her, I hated to think what would happen if Tania gave the ghost bad news about her husband. And my sister might have looked like a sweet little kid who could blow over in a strong breeze, but I knew better than to try to change her mind when she got that look.

Oh, well. If I was lucky, she was just crazy.

CHAPTER
12

I eyed Tania's ice cream. "Are you almost done? I don't know how anyone can eat so slowly."

She looked down at the paper cup. "It's mostly melted now, anyway. Let's go."

"All right. But if you're not going to eat that . . ." I grabbed the cup and slurped down the melted ice cream, with chunks of cookie dough at the bottom. Yum.

We left the store and started walking down Main Street. "I guess we have to go back to the hotel and ask some more questions." I yawned. The air felt hot and heavy. I just wanted to find a big park, stretch out on the grass, and sleep. It seemed like a really long day. And now, with the bright sun shining on all the pastel signs of girly little gift shops, it was hard to believe in ghosts. The world just wasn't that interesting.

"I wish I knew more about ghosts," Tania said. "I

would have done some research if I knew I was going to see one."

"Yeah, that does make a difference. There's probably all sorts of stuff on the Internet."

"That's it!" Tania said. "We ought to be able to find a computer somewhere here. They must have a public library."

Great. Doing research on vacation. But it made sense. "There's a business center at the hotel. I saw a thing about it in our room. We can borrow Mom's laptop. Tell her we want to check e-mail."

The wind had picked up, and Tania staggered as we climbed the hill toward the hotel. Dark clouds were piling up in the west. We found Bruce and Mom and the film crew filming the outside of the hotel.

"Bruce must be ecstatic," Tania said. I could barely hear her over the wind. "That will look great on film."

I had to admit, it was great atmosphere, with the dark bubbling clouds overhead and the wind whipping the bushes in front of the gray stone castle.

We edged up to Mom. Her hair was blowing all over. She gave us an absent glance, then focused more closely on Tania. "You shouldn't be out in this! You don't even have a jacket."

Despite the wind, it was still at least eighty-five degrees out, but I didn't bother to argue. "We were just heading inside. Thought we'd check e-mail, if we can borrow your computer."

Mom nodded. "Maggie knows where it is." She glanced at her watch. "When you're ready for dinner, just go to the hotel dining room. They'll put it on the show's account. We'll be out here for a while."

She got that look, the one that says she's starting to feel guilty about not being there for us. Since Tania and I didn't want company, I said, "Thanks. We're pretty worn out, so we'll probably keep it quiet this evening. Maybe watch TV." I gave her a hug, because that kind of thing makes her feel better.

She hugged Tania, too, and said, "I'll stop in to say good night. And maybe tomorrow we can do something together."

"Sure, if you're not too busy." I wasn't too worried. The TV show seemed to keep her hopping. I turned toward the hotel, and then remembered the ghost. I didn't want Tania to go past her again. "Let's go around back," I said. "We don't want to mess up the filming."

Unfortunately, Mom heard me. "You can go in the front. We're not filming right this minute."

Drat. I couldn't figure a good way out of the situation. I glanced at Tania, but she had her jaw set and she started toward the front door. What could I do but follow?

We pushed through the big doors. I found myself staring at the stairs, as if this time I would see the ghost myself. I guess I really had started to believe. And if ghosts were real, I wanted to see one.

I didn't see anything but a couple of guests going up with their suitcases.

And then it happened. This woman in a white wedding dress stepped out of the hallway at the top of the stairs.

My stomach lurched. I tried to tell myself it was just a real person getting married, but she didn't look right. The dress was old-fashioned, and she had her hair piled up in this fancy style. She seemed to reflect a bright light, but her face was too white, with dark circles under her eyes. She glided toward the stairs and started down slowly.

I couldn't take my eyes off her. I couldn't breathe.

I was actually seeing the ghost.

The room seemed to spin around me as I kept my eyes locked on to the ghost. Halfway down the stairs she stumbled and grabbed the banister. "Darn these shoes!" She hiked up her dress and adjusted her foot in a pair of white high heels.

The ghost looked past me and said, "Can't I just go barefoot? It will be easier to float."

I almost choked. I glanced to the corner and saw one

of the production assistants fiddling with a spotlight. He said, "Try it and we'll see. But hurry up; they should be done with the outside shots any minute."

I slumped back against the door and caught my breath. I couldn't believe I'd been fooled by an actress. She trotted up the stairs and around the corner.

"Come on," I muttered. I grabbed Tania's elbow and tried to drag her toward the dining room, but she shook me off.

"I want to speak to her," she whispered.

"She's just an actress. She doesn't know anything."

"Not *her*," Tania said. "Her!"

"What? Oh." The ghost was here too. For some reason, that really threw me. I wondered again if this was all some prank of Tania's. I guess I just didn't want to be fooled another time.

Tania's eyes seemed to follow something coming down the stairs. The actress reappeared at the top, presumably without her shoes.

My curiosity got the better of me. "Does she look anything like the actress?"

Tania's eyes flickered back and forth. "Not really. The actress is thinner and prettier, and the dress isn't right." She took a deep breath. "I'm going to talk to her."

"But I thought you couldn't understand her."

"I can't, but maybe she can understand me."

She was trembling and her breath came quick, but she held her ground. I glanced around and saw the desk clerk watching us. I gave him a quick smile and moved to block his view of Tania.

"We're trying to find out something about your husband," Tania whispered. "We want to help."

Tania held up her hand, then jerked it back as if she had touched a hot stove. She ducked her head, and her face twisted with pain or shock.

I grabbed her arm and jerked her away. She stumbled as I dragged her across the foyer. Her arm felt ice cold again, and her fingers were actually blue.

CHAPTER 13

The closest room was the business center, so I pulled Tania in there. Fortunately, it was empty, though the door stood open and the check-in desk was right on the other side. I held Tania's arm as I glanced back to the foyer. Of course I didn't see anything, except the desk clerk giving me a sour look.

I shook Tania gently. "Are you all right? She's not following, is she?"

Tania took a deep, shuddering breath and straightened up. Her voice trembled, but she said, "I'm okay." She looked back toward the stairs. "She's not following. She's still reaching out, but she seems to be stuck there. Poor thing."

I snorted. "That poor thing is really going to hurt you one of these times."

"She doesn't mean to. She's just—"

"I know, unhappy." I sighed. "Wait here. I'll get Mom's computer and we can get started."

Mostly the business center had laptop stations, but it did have one computer already set up. Tania got on that one, and I set up Mom's laptop a few feet away.

Tania stared at the screen and scrunched up her nose. "We're going to get millions of hits for ghosts. How do we figure out what's real?"

"Good question. Dad always says to look for government, university, or medical sites. But somehow I don't think that will help. I doubt the government has released studies on ghosts. I guess we just look around and see what we can find."

We turned up lots of hits, all right. It was hard to find anything useful. After about fifteen minutes, Tania groaned. "I can't believe this. Ghost sightings are bunched together with things like ESP, UFOs, Bigfoot, witches, and the Bermuda Triangle. I feel like a complete nutcase!"

I glanced at the desk clerk, who had turned to look in at us. "Shh!" I kept my voice low. "Just because you believe in one thing doesn't mean you have to believe in everything. Maybe it's like conspiracy theories. Some people just like to believe in conspiracies. But even if most of them are false, one of them could still be true."

She gave me a reluctant smile. "All right. But if I

start seeing little green aliens, just lock me up."

I was glad she still had her skepticism about other things. I was reading something about people who just want to believe. It was this essay saying that there's no evidence for paranormal phenomena. It said that some people are afraid to face death, so they come up with illusions that help them deal. Like ghosts are proof of an afterlife. It made me think uncomfortably of Mom.

It also had two questions you should ask someone who claimed he had seen a ghost, or whatever. Did it really happen like he said? And is his explanation the most likely one? In other words, maybe it was a hallucination or fantasy. Or maybe he really saw something, but not what he'd thought.

I glanced at Tania. She was usually pretty normal. Sure, she used to love fairy tales and act out imaginary life with her dolls or stuffed animals. But that's normal kid stuff. I didn't think she was what this guy called "fantasy prone."

I kept reading about science versus "pseudo-science." That's what a lot of people call psychic phenomenon—the belief in all those things Tania had mentioned. This guy seemed pretty smart, and he made some good points. He said that we assume the things we believe are true. Well, that seems obvious—if we didn't think they were true, we wouldn't believe them. But he pointed out that if we all really believed the Truth, we wouldn't have many disagreements. And of course people disagree all the time about everything, so a lot of what we call "truth" is really just our own personal belief.

Half an hour later, I had a headache. Lots of the sites I found were from believers, who usually sounded pretty flaky. The ones who sounded sensible mostly didn't believe in ghosts. Some of them were open-minded— they thought science should investigate ghosts more. I could agree with that. But lots of these people used so many big words and hard concepts that it was like listening to Dad talk about his work.

I had followed most of it—at least I think I did—but I hadn't found much that helped. Just that Tania was right: Lots of people would think she was lying, fantasizing, mistaken, or downright nuts if she claimed she could see ghosts.

Then there was the question about ghosts being dangerous. Some people saw ghosts and went crazy. Or were they crazy before seeing the ghost? Who knew? And then there were the people who claimed they were attacked.

I was staring at the computer screen, just thinking, when Tania jumped up from her chair and crouched next to me. The screen had stuff about how people who claim to see ghosts scored high on this "fantasy scale." I fumbled for the mouse, but Tania didn't notice. She was busy hissing in my ear.

"I was just reading about poltergeists, and it says they usually show up where there are children, especially preteen girls. So maybe I started seeing ghosts because I hit the right age!"

"Oh?" I had clicked back to the main search page, so I tried to take in what she was saying. "That means you'll stop seeing them someday, right? That would be good."

Tania frowned. "I'm not sure. It would be weird to stop seeing them, now that I know they're real." She glanced out the window, where some sparrows flapped in a tree. "Kind of like not being able to see birds anymore, but still knowing they exist."

That was a funny way to think about it. I wondered what I was missing. What strange things went on all around me, and I didn't even notice? Like the air is full of radio waves, but we can't see or feel them. What else was out there?

Tania bounced to the computer and started typing. "I'm going to see if I can find anything about girls who see ghosts."

I'd had about enough of research, but I typed in "poltergeist." Of course, the theories about them were all over the place. Maybe they were mischievous spirits. Maybe they were hoaxes, or the person was imagining things. Maybe they were static electricity, ball lightning or another physical thing. Maybe they were a result of psychokinesis.

I had to look up that one. Also called telekinesis, it means that the mind can do something physical—like move an object—without touching it. One theory said preteen girls had extra telekinetic power because of their hormones. They didn't just see poltergeists, they *caused* them. And poltergeists could do real damage.

Tania said, "I found this site where people share their psychic experiences! These other girls have written in, girls about my age. And several mothers wrote about their little children seeing ghosts. One of them said kids can see ghosts better because they're not held back by the logical adult mind."

"Tania," I groaned, "don't believe everything you read. Remember, we're trying to be scientific about this."

"But science doesn't know everything! They make new scientific discoveries all the time. Science used to think acupuncture was bunk, but now believes it can work for some things."

I wondered if she was quoting something she'd just read. "Well, at least let's be as scientific as we can."

She wrinkled her nose. "Easy for you to say! I'm

just glad I'm not the only one who sees ghosts."

I sighed. "Yeah." But why did she have to be one of the ones?

I'd had enough for one day. I went to the website where I could check my e-mail. A few nice, normal messages from friends back home might make me feel normal again too.

Tania got up and stretched. "I'm done. Are you ready to go?"

"Checking e-mail," I muttered.

She went out. I have to admit, I was glad to be alone for a while. I started reading these elephant jokes my aunt had forwarded. Each one was pretty dumb by itself, but somehow they built up over time. I was chuckling by the time I got to: *How do you know when there's an elephant under your bed?* Your nose is squashed against the ceiling.

It felt good to forget about ghosts and sisters and responsibilities, and just do regular stupid stuff.

Then I heard the scream.

CHAPTER

14

I was out of my seat before I realized I'd moved. As I leaped out the door, one thought filled my mind. Not Tania. That wasn't Tania's scream. Whoever it was, it wasn't Tania.

Still, my heart pounded and my stomach clenched. I pushed past the check-in desk. The desk clerk—she must've been the one who screamed—was hurrying to the bottom of the stairs.

Tania lay crumpled halfway down.

I thought I was going to be sick. It flashed through my mind all at once—what if something really happened to her? If she was badly hurt, or dead. The fear, the grief, we'd all go through again. Waiting in the hospital. Waiting for bad news.

And I should have been with her. I was supposed to watch out for her, now of all times, with everything going on. But I'd been tired of it all, and I'd let her down.

I passed the desk clerk on the stairs and fell to my knees beside Tania. My heart thudded so loud, I could hardly hear my own voice asking her if she was okay. She was already stirring, sitting up, but I had to hear her say it. Even as my eyes told me she couldn't be badly hurt, my heart couldn't quite believe.

"I'm all right." She pushed my hands away and sat up. "I'm fine."

The desk clerk babbled beside me. "I'll call the doctor. Your mother."

Tania grabbed her arm. "No, wait. I don't want everyone worrying about me."

"Honey, that was a bad fall!" The clerk put a hand to her chest. "I thought I was going to have a heart attack just watching you."

Tania met my eyes with a look that calmed me down more than her words. She was already thinking about how to get rid of the desk clerk, how to avoid Mom. My racing heart started to slow, and I tried to think with her.

"Where is everyone, anyway?"

The woman took a deep breath. She was still flushed and breathing fast, but maybe we could calm her down if we stayed calm enough. "They filmed that actress, and said they were done shooting for the day. They're having a meeting in the private dining room."

Excellent. "We'll just go in and tell Mom," I said. "You shouldn't leave the counter."

The woman reached for Tania. "But honey, you shouldn't move! You're supposed to stay still after a fall."

"I'm fine!" Tania stood up to prove it. She winced and grabbed the banister.

I jumped up beside her and took her arm. "She never listens to me, either," I told the clerk. "Don't worry, I'll make sure she's all right."

Since we started moving, there wasn't much the clerk could do. She trailed behind us and went back to the front counter, still looking worried. Tania and I stepped into the dining room. A few people were seated at tables. An open door at the back of the room led into the private dining room. I could see some of the TV crew inside.

"We're not really telling Mom, right?" Tania whispered.

"You're sure you're all right?"

"Yes."

"Absolutely positively sure?"

"Yes!"

"You made a face when you got up."

She made another face, but a different type. "I just turned my ankle when I fell, and kind of banged my knee. They feel fine now."

"All right, we won't tell."

I could feel Tania relax. "Okay. Now what?"

I glanced at my watch. "It's almost dinnertime. Let's eat."

"Don't you ever stop eating?"

"Not if I can help it. Anyway, we can't go back out there with the desk clerk watching."

A guy in a nice suit crossed the room toward us with a cool smile. "May I help you?"

"Two for dinner," I said. "Can we have a table that's out of the way? You know, private?"

He gave me a strange look—I guess he usually gets that question from romantic couples, and I hope that's not what he thought we were. Still, he gave us a table in the back corner of the dining room, away from most of the guests.

"What happened?" I asked.

She shrugged. "It's really not that big a deal. When I saw nobody was out there but that woman, I thought I'd take the chance to talk to the ghost again. I went up the stairs, and she was coming down to meet me."

She looked down, fumbling with her napkin. "I guess I lost my nerve. She had that horrible sad look, and she reached out for me. And I remembered how cold it was before. And you weren't there . . ."

Yeah, thanks for reminding me. It would take a while to work off the guilt from that one.

Tania looked up. "I wanted to get away. So I turned to run down the stairs, and tripped over my own feet."

I shuddered, thinking of Tania falling down those stairs. Had the ghost done the same, over a century ago? Was that what had killed her? If Tania's fall had been worse, would she have become another ghost, alongside this one?

Tania shrugged, her face pink. "It was stupid."

"No way. She scares *me*, and I can't even see her."

Tania smiled. "Thanks."

A waiter came with menus. Tania buried her face in hers. I stared out the tall windows. Trees thrashed in the wind, and the low sun glared through gaps in the dark clouds. Now it was easy to believe in ghosts. Who would've thought weather made such a difference?

The waiter came back to take our order, so I shook off the mood and asked for a hamburger and French fries. Tania got lasagna.

We watched the waiter leave, then finally looked at each other. "Are you sure you want to keep doing this?" I said.

"I have to." She turned her napkin in her hands. "This is going to sound weird."

"Compared to the rest of today?"

She gave me half a smile. "Every time the ghost

touches me, it's like—like I understand her better. Like she's putting part of herself into me."

That didn't just sound weird, it sounded scary. Like possession.

"I have to help her," Tania went on. "If I leave without helping her, I'll always feel like I left some part of me here with her."

CHAPTER
15

I swallowed hard. My skin felt clammy. I wondered again if I should be doing this—helping Tania instead of keeping her away from the ghost. But I didn't know what else to do. It felt like we'd come too far to turn back.

I took a deep breath. "All right. So what do we do?"

She frowned. "We need to find out what happened to her husband. But how?"

We had a question. We needed an answer. "We do what Dad would do," I said. "We start with a hypothesis, and work from there."

Tania nodded slowly. "You mean, we come up with a guess about what happened, and then test it?"

"Exactly. But we call it a hypothesis because it sounds more important and will make us feel like we're making progress."

That got a real smile. "All right," Tania said. "The

question is, what happened to the groom? He disappeared on his wedding night. Why would he?"

"Maybe he changed his mind? Got cold feet?"

Tania scrunched up her nose. "It doesn't seem likely. He could have disappeared before the wedding, or refused to say 'I do.' Waiting until the wedding night just seems mean."

"He had a nasty sense of humor?"

Tania sighed. "Maybe he did. But that doesn't help us. We need an explanation that we can investigate."

The waiter brought our food. Tania slowly chewed a nibble of lasagna. She took a sip of water and wiped her mouth with a napkin. I was already halfway done with my burger.

"It would help if we knew more about them," I mumbled.

Tania gave me a disgusted look. "Gross. Finish chewing before you talk."

I swallowed. "If we had names, we might be able to find records."

"I don't think the ghost is going to be able to tell me her name." Tania picked at her food. "I wish Dad were here. He knows about research."

"We could call him. Ask for some advice. But you said you didn't want him to know you'd seen a ghost."

Tania frowned and nodded. "Maybe we could still

get some help. We don't have to tell him exactly why we want to know."

"Good point. We'll just say we're curious because of the TV show, and want to know how he would go about it, as a scientist."

After dinner, we went up to our hotel suite and into my bedroom to call Dad. I dialed and held the phone to my ear. "Dad? It's Jon."

"Hey! How are you? Is everything all right?"

"Sure, we're good. We just thought we'd call to chat. Tania's here too."

Tania was leaning over the phone with her back to me. I couldn't see what she was doing. Suddenly a loud beep just about shattered my eardrum. I jumped. Dad's voice was now coming out of the speakerphone. "—been wondering how you guys were doing on the TV set."

"Oh, it's great," Tania said. "Hi, Dad, we have you on speakerphone now." She smirked at me and whispered, "I'm no good with technology, huh?"

I glared at her and hung up the handset. We both turned our attention to what Dad was saying.

"Hi, sweetheart! So you're having fun?"

"Oh sure," I muttered, rubbing my ear. "It's a blast."

"It's fun seeing how they put the TV show together," Tania said. "Bruce did some interviews this morning. This one lady seemed really nice, but kind of ordinary, like my second-grade teacher, Mrs. Fiske? Only Bruce thought her story was boring. And then he interviewed this woman who called herself a psychic. All red hair and red lips and attitude. I thought she seemed phony, but Bruce said she looked good on camera."

"See, that's the problem with those kinds of shows," Dad said. "It's all about what looks good, or makes a good sound bite. They don't use rigorous testing, so scientists can never take them seriously."

This was just the opportunity we were looking for. "So, Dad, what would you do to investigate ghosts, as a scientist?"

He laughed. "I wouldn't bother. You know I don't believe in nonsense like that."

"But, Dad," I said, "you know that's not good science. Aren't you supposed to be open-minded about things? No one has proven ghosts *don't* exist, right?"

After a pause, he said, "You're right. You can't prove a negative. But I have no reason to believe they do exist. In fact, I *can't* believe in ghosts. Even if I wanted to, I just couldn't make myself believe something like that. Maybe that is bad science, because it becomes a matter of faith. But my beliefs are as strong as your mother's, even if they are different."

I didn't want to get into that. "But if you did believe—or even if you didn't, and wanted to disapprove ghosts—say you wanted to investigate them. How would you, as a scientist, do it?"

He was silent for a minute, and I thought he wasn't going to answer. Tania perched on the edge of the bed and gazed at me, her hands clenched in her lap.

I guess he was just thinking. "I gather that there are supposed to be different types of ghosts. The easiest type to test would be a ghost that appears at the same point on some regular schedule. Then you try capture that manifestation. If it's visual, you use video cameras. If it's audible, you use tape recorders. But not just one. Sound on a single tape recorder could be anything. You put several around the house, to weed out background noise, like the water heater bubbling. You should only get a recording where you hear the ghost. And you need a time-tag, to make sure the recording is right when the ghost was supposed to appear."

Tania gave me a small smile. "So if we did that, and got a recording, you'd believe in ghosts?"

Dad laughed. "No, I admit that I wouldn't. I'd probably have to see one with my own eyes, and even then I'd try to figure out what the trick was."

Tania sighed. I gave her a sympathetic shrug. Neither of us had really believed we'd convince Dad.

I tried to come up with questions that might help

us, without giving away why we wanted to know. "So . . . if ghosts existed, do you have any idea of what they would be?"

"Hmmm. No, I really don't. It just falls too far outside of anything that I've considered. I know ghost hunters sometimes use those electromagnetic detectors. That would suggest a ghost is an electromagnetic imprint from the dead person. But electromagnetic structures aren't very long-lived. It's pretty far-fetched."

"You mean the fields would fade quickly, once someone was gone?"

"Right. They don't even last after you leave the room." He was silent for a minute, and then went on. "The hard part is, how you investigate ghosts is going to depend on what you assume about them. If you assume that they are trapped in a cycle, and only do what they have been observed to do in the past, that makes things easier. But if they're self-willed, they could play tricks and throw off the evidence."

Fortunately, I was used to him talking like that. "You mean a ghost could play a joke by messing with your equipment?"

Tania chimed in. "Bruce said ghosts are hard to photograph. They mess up the film."

"Right," Dad said. "So are the ghosts playing hard to get? Or do ghosts have a form that doesn't show up on film? Or is it all just trick photography, a hoax? How can we tell?"

"Well, how *can* we tell?" I asked.

"Keep your eyes and ears open when you're on the set. Maybe you'll be able to tell me."

Tania leaned toward the phone. "So what would you do if a ghost appeared to you?"

Dad laughed. "Probably stand there staring like an idiot. But I'd be intrigued. I might set up some of these experiments and look for a pattern for the ghost. But I don't expect it to happen."

It was funny how different his response was from Tania's. She didn't care about understanding the ghost, except to help her. I shook myself and tried to get back on track. "But what if the ghost couldn't talk? I mean, what if you saw a ghost, but you didn't know how to talk to it?"

"That's a lot of ifs." I could hear the smile in Dad's voice.

"Yeah, well, that's what a lot of science is, right?"

"Okay. You're really making me think here tonight. Let's see. If it's just a misty thing floating there, that's not a whole lot of help. If it's a ghost that just goes through the same set of repeated actions, perhaps you can deduce something from that. If it can't talk but it can see and react to what's around it, you might be able to communicate through gestures."

Ghost sign language. It had possibilities, but I wasn't sure what.

"You're really getting into this ghost stuff, aren't you?" Dad said.

I shrugged, then realized he couldn't see me. "It's kind of interesting. It gives us something to do."

"Just make sure you maintain your skepticism," Dad said. "I know I've told you to keep an open mind, but don't believe everything you hear."

"Or see?" Tania whispered, just loud enough for me to hear.

"I wouldn't even let you travel with the show," Dad went on, "if I thought they were going to brainwash you into believing all that junk."

"No, it's cool," I said. "No one's trying to convince us of anything. Even Bruce says it's okay for me to be skeptical."

"It really is fun," Tania said, "seeing how they put the TV show together. Maggie, the production assistant— Mom asked her to look after us—she was telling us about her job today, when we went for ice cream in town."

"Wait a minute," Dad said, "who's looking after you?"

"Her name is Maggie and she's really nice. You'd like her." Tania smirked at me. "Jon sure does."

I felt myself blushing. Dad said, "I agreed to let you travel with the show so you could spend more time with your mother and Bruce. I'm not sure I like the idea of this other person taking care of you. And if she's an employee of the show, doesn't she have other duties?"

"We don't need a babysitter," I said. "I'm thirteen! I can look after both of us."

"Maybe so," Dad said. "But that's not really the point. You're supposed to be spending time with your mother, not running around on your own, or with some stranger."

"We do see Mom," Tania said. "We saw her a bunch of times today. She said maybe we'd do some sightseeing together tomorrow."

"Tomorrow." I could hear the frown in Dad's voice. "This is what I was afraid of. She says she wants to spend time with you, but then she gets wrapped up in her job. I barely watch TV, but even I know working on a show must be a twenty-four-hour-a-day job when you're on the set. If you're not spending time together, maybe you'd be better off here. You could lead a normal life, hang out with your friends."

Tania's eyes were huge with panic. "Oh, no! We're getting a lot out of this. It's really educational. We'll get to see more of the country, and learn things and meet new people. And we do get to spend time with Mom. We're going to spend more together, I promise."

"Hmm. Well, you let me know if that doesn't work out. Remember, you can come home anytime you want."

A week ago that might have sounded pretty good. But now I wanted to know what would happen next. And it would kill Tania to leave without helping her ghost. "Really, Dad, it's cool," I said. "We're having a good time. Don't worry about us."

Tania turned her head suddenly and went white, like she was seeing a ghost again. But when I turned, I could see it too—Mom. She was standing in the doorway, hands on her hips and a scowl on her face.

"Um, gotta go, Dad," I said. "Thanks for the, um, ideas."

"Well, call anytime, you know that. I love you two."

"I love you," Tania chirped, still staring at Mom.

I looked toward the phone, away from Mom. "Yeah, love you," I mumbled.

Tania clicked off the phone. Our eyes met. How much had Mom heard?

She came into the room. "Well! So I'm not spending enough time with you. Is that what he thinks? Is that what *you* think?"

"No, Mom," I said.

"It's been great!" Tania said. "We've had a really good time. And we *have* seen you today, you know that."

Mom sighed, and her anger seemed to fade. "Just for a few minutes here and there. And mostly I've been distracted." She put her arms around Tania. "Honey, you fainted this morning, and I couldn't even stay with you! I was too busy with the show. Oh, what kind of mother am I?"

"You're the best mother," Tania said, hugging her hard.

I groaned silently, got up, and went to put my arms around Mom too. "You don't have to feel bad about anything. We've had an, um . . . amazing day."

"With Magdalene! A stranger, and not your own mother." Mom sniffled.

"We know you're busy. It's all right," Tania said. "We'll have lots of time together."

Mom straightened and brushed the tears from her eyes. "That's right, you will. Tomorrow! The show can survive perfectly well without me for one day. Everything's set up, anyway." She beamed at us. "Tomorrow, I'm spending the whole day with my kids!"

Tania and I exchanged a glance and forced smiles onto our faces. Great. There's nothing like a guilty mom to mess up your plans.

CHAPTER 16

Over breakfast, Mom asked us what we wanted to do that day. "We could just stay around here," I suggested. "Watch the filming." I figured that was the best way to keep up our ghost research without attracting attention.

"Oh no," Mom said. "If they see me, they'll expect me to work. Let's walk through the town. I hear it's adorable."

Tania and I looked at each other and shrugged. At least it was a small town. Maybe Mom would get bored soon.

We walked down the same way we had gone with Maggie. I thought about suggesting ice cream again, but figured Mom would say it was too early in the day. She's funny that way.

"Look!" The excitement in Tania's voice made me jump. I thought she must have seen another ghost.

I looked where she was pointing, but all I saw was another building with an old-fashioned sign. The sign read HISTORICAL SOCIETY MUSEUM.

"Let's go in!" Tania said.

I groaned. "We're on vacation and you want to go to a museum? Don't you get enough history in school?"

Tania rolled her eyes. As Mom peered at the sign, Tania whispered to me, "They might know something about the ghost!"

Oh, right. She scurried to the door and I followed her.

We entered a small, dimly lit room. A woman with short, fluffy gray hair sat behind the counter on our left. A rack of brochures slumped on the right. Old photos hung on the walls.

The woman said, "Welcome. May I help you?"

Tania stepped forward and placed a hand on the counter. Old ladies always like her, and I waited to see how she'd get the info she wanted from this one.

"Hi! We're with the TV crew at the hotel. You know, the ones doing the ghost show?"

I almost choked. I had been expecting something more subtle.

The lady just smiled. "Oh, how nice. But you look a little young. Are you actors?"

"No, our mom is a producer." Mom introduced herself, and they chatted for a few minutes.

I pulled Tania aside. "How are we going to do this?"

"We can be interested in the ghost's story, right? It just makes sense." She joined Mom and the lady. "I suppose you've heard about the Ghost Bride. Can you tell us anything about her?"

"People have different theories about who she was, but nobody knows for sure. She's supposed to be from the late 1800s, but even that isn't definite."

"What about her wedding dress?" Tania asked. "Wouldn't that help tell when she's from?"

The lady chuckled. "Only if you could actually see the ghost, and see what her dress looked like. People don't always agree on what they've seen. They talk about 'a lady in white,' but actually white wasn't a common color for wedding dresses back then. I suspect those people hear about a Ghost Bride, assume a white dress, and then see what they want to see. In any case, style can only tell you so much. This isn't New York City. It might have taken a few years for styles to make their way west. The dress might have been outdated already."

Tania looked fascinated. Maybe she was. She opened her eyes wide. "Do you have any books or old photos of wedding clothes back then?"

The lady pulled a book out from under the counter, and soon she, Tania, and Mom were buried in it. As they critiqued wedding dresses through the ages, I looked at the brochures. I found one for hot-air balloons. Now that would be cool, but I didn't have to be psychic to know it wasn't in my future.

"I really like this one," Tania said. "Look, Jon!"

"Yeah, nice," I said, glancing at the book from about five feet away. Tania gave me a significant look and I realized what she was doing. I went closer and checked out the picture. It was pretty much like the dress Tania had described, and sure enough, it was from the 1890s.

"I guess you'd have to be pretty rich to afford something fancy like that," Tania said.

"Oh yes," the museum lady said. "Ordinary people just wore a nice, new dress when they got married. Then they could use it for other special occasions, like church or parties."

They finished ogling the dresses, and Tania turned her big, innocent eyes on the museum lady. "It seems really strange that the ghost's husband just disappeared," Tania said. "How could that happen?"

"It would be easy, actually." The woman got up. You could hardly tell the difference, because she wasn't any taller standing then she had been sitting. She waddled out from behind the counter and I realized she was wearing an old-fashioned dress. Not just out of date, but really old-fashioned, with a skirt that reached the floor, and poofy white lace under her chin. The top was so tight, I didn't know how she could breathe.

Tania said, "Wow, I like your dress!"

I gaped at her, then snapped my mouth shut. It must have been part of her plan to make a good impression.

The lady actually curtsied. "Why, thank you, my dear." She waddled across the room and gestured toward the wall. "Look at these photographs. This might be a nice little touristy town now, but you see here that a century ago it was a crowded city of tenement buildings and saloons. Remember, this was still the Wild West back then."

I checked out the pictures. Sure enough, they showed crowded, narrow streets nothing like the current town. Even in the black-and-white photos, you could tell the stores didn't have lavender and mint green paint.

"Almost twenty thousand people lived here," the lady said. "And remember, people didn't have driver's licenses or Social Security cards."

She smiled up at me. "You could have walked into town and said you were Billy the Kid, nineteen years old, from Texas, and nobody could have proven otherwise!"

"I don't think I'd want to risk it," I joked. "Didn't people try to kill Billy the Kid?"

"They sure did! He only lived to be twenty-one. That wasn't so unusual back then. People lived fast and died young. By fourteen or fifteen you were considered an adult. You worked on the farm or in the family business."

She smiled at Tania. "Or got married and started having children, and took care of the kids, cleaned the house, did all the cooking—including baking bread from scratch in a wood-burning stove—and probably kept a garden and raised some hens. If a quiet, hardworking life didn't appeal to you, or if you didn't have a family to help you get started, you might take to the road. And you might wind up here. Gamblers, fortune hunters, con men, you name it. People came for a few years—or months or only days—and moved on."

Tania frowned. "So there's no way to figure out where he went, even if you knew his name?"

"If he didn't want to be found, no one would find him. The question is, why wouldn't he want to be found?"

We looked at the pictures for a few minutes while the lady babbled. "After the silver boom faded, the town got pretty run-down. The population dropped to four thousand, and a lot of the abandoned buildings started to fall apart. Twenty years ago the town council decided to revitalize and try to attract tourists. They tore down the crumbling buildings, rebuilt a few of the best ones, and filled in the gaps with new buildings meant to look old."

"Are they the ones who turned the hotel into a fake castle?" I asked.

"No, that was the original owner. It was built as a mansion by a mining baron. He was a local boy, but must've thought the English look made him seem more important. It was turned into a hotel after he died in 1893. If the Ghost Bride and her husband really honey-mooned there, they were probably two of the early guests."

Mom asked a question, and I escaped. Tania was studying the photos intently. I wasn't sure what she was looking for, but she peered at one and gasped. Mom and the museum lady were deep in conversation and didn't notice. "What's up?" I asked.

"It's her!"

"You're kidding." I leaned in and studied the picture. It was an old black-and-white photo of a young woman in a long dress. It was kind of blurry, with cracked marks. I wasn't positive I would recognize the woman if I saw her on the street, but Tania was nodding.

"I'm sure it's her. But who is she?"

The label below the photo just said, "A young local woman, circa 1890."

"That's not much help," I said. "Wait a minute—what's this on the picture?" We peered at the picture from a few inches away, trying to make out the words. "Miss Stevers?" I suggested.

"Or Stevens. Or maybe even Sterens or Steves." Tania put her hands on her hips and wrinkled her nose. "Why couldn't that photographer have better handwriting!"

"What are you two so interested in?" Mom asked.

I jumped back from the photo. I'd forgotten she was there. "Oh, nothing. Just, um . . ."

"More dresses!" Tania said perkily. "I really like these old styles. I wish we still dressed like that."

Mom smiled and brushed Tania's hair back from her eyes. "You don't know how nice it is to hear that, when so many of these young girls are dressing in next to nothing. Maybe we can look for some long dresses for you."

I chuckled. If Tania didn't watch out, she was going to be dressed up like an old-fashioned doll.

Tania kept her smile. "Oh, I suppose jeans are more comfortable. But it's fun to dress up once in a while."

I'd had about enough of the museum. "Ready to go? Maybe we could get some lunch."

"Jonathan, it's only ten o'clock!" Mom said.

"Second breakfast, then."

She shook her head at me.

Tania said, "I have an idea! Let's look for the cemetery."

We all turned to stare at her.

"It might be a good place for filming, don't you think?" Tania's innocent act was working overtime. "We could check it out for the show."

I put on my best smile. "Sounds great to me!"

CHAPTER
17

The cemetery was on a hill outside of town. It was pretty big, which seemed strange for such a small town. Then I remembered the museum lady saying that twenty thousand people had lived here. I guess over the years, even a smallish town produces a lot of bodies.

Mom sighed and paused to look out over the grassy lawn and white tombstones. "It's pretty," she said.

I leaned closer to Tania and whispered, "So what are we looking for?"

"Her grave! Maybe it will tell us something."

I wasn't sure what a tombstone was supposed to tell us. It wasn't going to say, "Went mad and died because her husband abandoned her." It would probably just have her name and birth and death dates. I guess if she died in the 1890s, it would support Tania's identification. If not . . . well, I wasn't sure what that would mean.

We followed Mom as she wandered through the

newer part of the cemetery. Once in a while she studied a particular tombstone and sighed or murmured. I realized they were mostly the ones of children, and knew she was thinking of Angela. Maybe this wasn't such a good idea.

Tania had a funny look as well, and was sticking really close to me again. She kept glancing over her shoulder. I let Mom get about ten feet ahead. "What's up?" I whispered. Then it hit me. "Um . . . is anybody here?"

"I'm not sure. It so bright out, I can't see clearly. But I keep getting the feeling I see movement, or something shimmering."

I took a deep breath. "Let's pretend it's just heat shimmering off the stones. That'll make it easier to get through this."

She nodded and we caught up with Mom. This was getting too weird. I didn't think I could drag them away quite yet, but we could at least get away from the newer graves, the ones that looked like Angela's. "Hey, if we're looking for a good spot for the TV show to shoot, shouldn't we be in the older graves? This ghost is supposed to be like a hundred years old, right?"

Mom looked up and seem to shake off her mood. She smiled. "You're right, of course. Sorry I got distracted." She linked her arm through Tania's. "How about we try over there?"

Tania nodded, and we headed for the older-looking tombstones. We passed the 1950s graves. By the 1910s, some of the tombstones were so worn that it was hard to read the dates. Then we got to tombstones that were broken in half and lying on the ground. I had to bend down and run my finger over the numbers carved on them.

"1843, I think. We've gone too far back now." I pointed to the left. "Those don't seem quite so old."

Finally we found the right area. The tombstones were worn and moldy looking, but we could mostly make out the writing. "It does have . . . atmosphere," Mom said doubtfully. "But do you think this would really work in the show?"

Tania started walking down a row of graves, scanning the headstones. "Well, maybe the camera can pan over some of these, you know, the ones with names of young women who died about the right time? And Bruce could say something like, 'Could one of these have been the woman who became the Ghost Bride?'"

"That's not a bad idea." Mom chuckled. "I'm going to have to get you put on the TV staff!"

"So we just have to find tombstones with women's names, and she should be, what—eighteen, twenty? When did they get married back then?"

"Well, probably no younger than sixteen," Mom

said. "And twenty-five at the oldest, unless it was a second marriage. And she's supposed to be from the 1890s, or there about. So let's look for headstones of women who died between the ages of sixteen and twenty-five, sometime in the 1890s."

Tania grinned at me. I had to admit, the way she had led Mom on was perfect. We split up and started scanning the rows. Of course, Tania and I were really looking for the name Stevens or something similar, but Mom didn't have to know about that. I had to remind myself to check for other graves that would fit her criteria.

"Here's one!" she called out, gazing at a big marble tombstone with an angel on it. "Rose McGloin, twenty-two years old. Must have been rich, with this fancy headstone. Should we be marking them somehow? We might have a hard time finding them again. But I didn't bring any flagging tape, and, anyway, that seems kind of . . . not respectful."

"Maybe we could make a map," I said.

"Great idea!" Mom fished in her purse. "Good thing I always carry this notebook. Let's see . . . I'll count the number of rows in this section, and mark a few landmarks, like that tree. Then we just have to note how far along the right graves are in each row. I'll start mapping this one, and you two call out if you find anything else."

Forty minutes later, Mom said, "I think that's all of

them from the right years. We have a few, anyway."

I looked at Tania. She shrugged and shook her head. We had found a couple of gravestones for people named Stevens, but they were all wrong. Men, or older women, and one little girl. We hadn't found any of the other possible variations of the name. So unless they got the dates wrong on the headstone, our Miss Stevens wasn't here.

Then it hit me and I groaned. I muttered to Tania, "What idiots we are! She was married. She wouldn't have been buried as a Stevens."

Tania's mouth dropped open. "Oh! Of course you're right. The marriage didn't last very long, but back in those days it wouldn't have mattered. She was married, so she was a Mrs."

"The name Stevens doesn't help us at all."

"So we *have* to find out who she married," Tania said. "What a waste of time. We could at least have been looking for men's graves."

"Even harder. We don't know his name, and he might have been older when he married."

Mom snapped her notebook shut, stuck it in her purse, and came toward us.

"I wonder if there really are ghosts here," Tania said. "Maybe I could talk to some of them—"

"Not now," I said, turning to smile at Mom. "Well, that was fun. Is it lunchtime yet?"

CHAPTER
18

We stopped at a sandwich shop. After we'd ordered, Tania said, "Wouldn't it be great if we could figure out who the ghost really was?"

Mom smiled indulgently. "It would be lovely, but other people have tried. The woman at the historical museum told me that several of the locals have theories about the ghost, but none of them can prove they're right."

"Well," Tania said, "maybe we could find some information they don't have." She smiled brightly and I tried to keep from laughing, knowing what information she already had.

Mom was having a hard time not laughing too, but for a different reason. "Research takes a lot of time, darling. We're just here today and part of tomorrow."

"We could at least try," Tania said, her eyes wide. "It would be fun!"

Mom thanked the waiter as he put down our sandwiches, and then she turned back to Tania. "All right,
what did you have in mind?"

"Old newspapers. We look for announcements of
weddings from the right time, then compare them to the
names of the women who died young, from the tombstones."

I thought it was a pretty clever idea, but Mom
frowned. "Will they have newspaper records from
back then? Did this town even have a newspaper back
then?"

"They did," I said. "I remember seeing a couple of
front pages posted in the historical society. They were
from before 1900."

"Well, that's something," Mom said. "But still, they
might not have complete records. I don't even know if
they would have posted wedding announcements back
then."

"We can at least try," Tania said.

"That's really how you'd like to spend your afternoon
with me?"

Tania nodded, her big eyes pleading. Mom turned to
me, and I nodded as well, my mouth full of sandwich.

"All right, then! We have a plan."

As we ate, we debated between trying the library,
the historical society, and the newspaper office. We

settled on the historical society, since that's where I had seen the old pages.

A different woman was on duty, taller and younger, but still wearing an old-fashioned dress. Hers was bright purple with lots of white lace and a big purple feather that bobbed above her head. Mom explained our mission.

"Yes, we do have old newspapers on file, on microfilm. We haven't completed all the transfers, but we have the ones from the earlier years, up to 1912. It was a weekly back then. Some weeks are missing, but they may just not have printed every week. Nothing was too predictable back then."

"We can look at them, then?" Mom asked.

"Sure, come into the back room. We call it our research library." She led the way, her purple feather waving like a flag.

I nudged Tania. "Microfilm? These people are as outdated as their clothes."

The room was small and dingy. Two walls had shelves covered with books. Another had a big cabinet with drawers only a couple of inches high. A short counter held a sink and coffeemaker. The lady offered Mom coffee, but she took one sip, coughed, and put it aside.

They only had one microfilm reader, so Tania sat in front of it. The lady pointed out a drawer with rolls of film labeled by year. I would bring them out one at a time, and Tania could skim through them while Mom and I looked over her shoulder. I expected this to get old quickly.

It took Tania a few minutes to get the hang of the microfilm reader, but soon she was going so fast, my eyes blurred. The newspapers' front pages mostly had national or world news reports, or big events like bank robberies. But inside they often had a column of social happenings. These included church socials, the occasional coming-out party, and yes, marriages.

Mom dutifully wrote down the names. "I wish I'd written down the names from the tombstones. Then we'd only have to compare against that, instead of listing all of these."

"We could go back there and then come back here," I suggested. Anything to get out of that stuffy room.

Tania's eyes never left the screen. "No, we're here. I've already gone through a year. This won't take too long."

I sighed and leaned back against the counter. We obviously had different definitions of too long. I wondered what Maggie was doing. Something more interesting than this, no doubt. Too bad we hadn't told her about our research plans. Maybe she would have helped.

I was daydreaming, not really paying attention, when

I heard Tania make a sound. Her hand had dropped away from the controls on the machine. I roused myself. "Ready for the next one?"

"It's her," she whispered.

I stepped over to look, as Mom peered closer. This one had rated a real news story, and even had a picture. Sure enough, it looked like the photo of Miss Stevens—blurry and faded. I wondered if that was the only reason Tania thought this was the ghost, because she was blurry and faded too.

Tania read aloud. "Rose Stevens to marry Frank McGloin this Saturday. Miss Stevens is the daughter of First City banker Joseph Stevens, and his wife, Ethel, known for her fine garden parties. Frank McGloin is a prospector, recently arrived in town, who made his money gold-panning. They will honeymoon at the recently opened Hilltop Hotel. The couple plan to reside here in town."

"Interesting," Mom said. "But how do you know it's our ghost? Is it because they were supposed to honeymoon at the hotel? Lots of couples might have done that."

"It's just a feeling I have," Tania said.

The museum lady had been hanging around, since no one else was in the building. "The Stevens were an important family back then. They had lots of money.

That's probably why the wedding was covered in the paper. I don't remember hearing the name McGloin before, though. It's not a common name around here."

Mom leaned back in her chair. "Wait a minute. There's something familiar about that name. McGloin . . . I just have a feeling I've heard that recently. Maybe on one of the tombstones this morning?"

"You see!" Tania said, bouncing in her chair. "It is her! Do you remember what else the tombstone said?"

Mom shook her head. "No, and I could be wrong. It could have been Mc-something else. And, anyway, it might have been on one of the newer tombstones I was looking at first. I'm not sure it was one of the young women who died in the 1890s."

"We have to go back and check!" Tania said. "And we can try to figure out what happened to Frank. Why would he abandon his new bride on their wedding night?"

"That is the real mystery," Mom said. "If he had recently arrived, they couldn't have known each other long, so he didn't have much time to get tired of her."

The museum lady pitched in. "Her family had money, but he never turned up to claim her inheritance, so it doesn't sound like he planned the whole thing."

They all stared at one another, frowning.

"He was kidnapped?" I suggested. "Captured by Indians? Eaten by a bear?"

Tania nodded slowly.

"You don't really think he was eaten by a bear?" I demanded.

Tania rolled her eyes. "Of course not. But I do think he might have been killed. That's the only thing that makes sense. He didn't come back because he couldn't. If he was injured, he would have turned up eventually, or sent a message. If he'd been kidnapped, they would have gotten a ransom note. So he was killed."

I had to admit, I couldn't think of a better hypothesis.

"He must have died on his wedding day," Tania said, "or within a few days, if he had an injury that killed him slowly. We can look for death notices over the next week or so, and see if Frank shows up." Her hand went back to the controls, and microfilm started sliding past on the screen. She found a few mentions of men who died. One got run over by a horse-drawn buggy while crossing the street, two didn't mention the cause of death, and one guy died in a shootout, of all things. But no Frank McGloin. A couple of the men were unidentified, though.

Tania sat back and wrinkled her nose. "I guess that makes sense. If they knew he died, they would have told Rose. But one of the unknowns could have been him. Funny that there were three in the next week."

The museum lady was interested now, and hanging over Tania's shoulder. "Not really. People came and went all the time. If he was new in town, probably few people knew him."

"And he might not have had any ID," I said, remembering what the other museum lady had told us.

"Let go back to the cemetery and look for Rose McGloin's tombstone," Tania said. "Then we can try to find graves for any men where they didn't know the name. I wonder how they would be labeled."

"Or if," I said. "Why would they even bother with a headstone? They probably just dumped them in a big unmarked grave."

Tania winced. "Well, we won't know unless we look."

Mom had been watching Tania, not the microfilm screen. "It's a delightful theory, dear, but don't you think you're getting a little too . . . involved? All this about death and graves!"

Tania turned to her, her face wide-eyed and serious for a moment, before she remembered to relax and smile. "It's just for fun! And if we can help the TV show—"

Mom shook her head. "The show is my responsibility, not yours. I'll mention this to Bruce, and he can follow up if he thinks it's important. But I think it's time to get out of here and have some fun! What do you say we go shopping?"

Honestly, even without the question of the ghost, I'd probably find a walk through the cemetery more fun than shopping with my mother and sister. But Mom seemed to be worrying about something, and Tania couldn't change her mind. We got a printout of the article on Rose and Frank McGloin and thanked the museum lady. Then Tania and I trailed after Mom, ready to have some "fun."

CHAPTER 19

Mom dragged us through a series of touristy gift shops. Tania managed to *ooh* and *ahh* over useless cute stuff, but I could tell she wasn't really into it. She was trying to figure out how to get Mom back to the cemetery.

"Leave it," I whispered, "if you don't want Mom to get suspicious."

"But we're running out of time!" she hissed. "The show packs up tomorrow. If we don't find out what happened soon, we may never know."

For my own sake, I could shrug that off. I was curious, but it didn't really matter if I never found out the truth. But it meant a lot to Tania. I tried to think of anything that might help. But after an hour in the back room of the museum, and three tacky gift shops, my brain was fried. I trailed after them, wishing I were anywhere else.

Then it hit me: that could be the excuse to get rid of

Mom. As she reached for the door of a candle shop, I sank down onto the edge of a stone planter with a loud sigh. "I'll wait here," I said in my best bored teen voice.

Mom hesitated. "I'm sorry, Jonathan. I guess this isn't much fun for you."

I shrugged. "I'm just tired. Maybe I'll go back to the hotel and watch TV or something." I tried to give Tania a meaningful glance, but it was hard with Mom watching me. Fortunately, she caught on quickly.

"I'm pretty tired too," she said with a little yawn. "I guess I haven't quite recovered from fainting yesterday."

That did it. Mom was bustling us up the street toward the hotel before I even had time to blink.

When we reached the hotel, Mom pushed on the doors, but they wouldn't open. She peered through the glass panes and shoved.

Finally the door opened a crack. The mean guy who had scolded us when we were watching the show earlier peered out. His scowl lifted slightly when he saw Mom. "Oh, hi, Annette, it's you. Sorry, they're playing with the lighting, and I was trying to keep out the nosy people."

"Come on, Mick, this is a place of business," Mom snapped. "You can't keep out customers."

"I've been sending them around to the side door," Mick said with a satisfied smile.

Mom pushed past him and led us inside. Bruce

waved and jogged over to give her a kiss on the cheek. He draped one arm over her shoulder and one over Tania's. "Did you girls have a good time in town?"

"We think we found out who the ghost is!" Tania said. "Show him, Mom."

Mom smiled and took the photocopy out of her purse. "Tania thinks this Rose Stevens could be the Ghost Bride."

Bruce took the paper and scanned it. "Hmm, definite possibilities. It's the right era, anyway. I don't see how we could possibly be sure, though."

The so-called psychic seemed to appear from nowhere. "I'd like to take a look." She plucked the paper out of Bruce's hands. "No, no, all wrong. This is not the woman I saw."

Tania scowled at her. "You didn't—" She stopped. "I mean, maybe she looks different, now that she's a ghost." She turned to Bruce. "We could look for her tombstone and see if she died in 1894. That would be pretty good evidence, right? And it would be better for the show, having a real person with a real name, don't you think, even if you're not one hundred percent sure?"

The psychic said, "Once I've had a chance to talk to the ghost, I can ask her her name."

"If she'll talk to you," Tania said. "Maybe she can't talk."

"I have already heard her speak."

That's right, the psychic had made that claim yesterday. Tania looked ferocious, but of course she couldn't call the psychic a liar. "Well, maybe she just repeats the same pattern and can't communicate. Didn't you say that before she disappeared right after she spoke? Maybe that's all she does."

The psychic raised one eyebrow. "I feel sure I shall be able to break through the barrier."

Bruce said, "We're looking forward to shooting a scene with Madame Natasha tomorrow morning. I was hoping to get to it today, but we had some camera trouble, and now it's getting late."

Tania didn't seem to be listening anymore. She gazed past Madame Natasha, at the stairs, and said clearly, "Well, I think the ghost's name is Rose Stevens. Or Rose McGloin, if you want her married name, when she died. Maybe that's what she'll tell you."

"It's possible," Madame Natasha said with a superior smile. "You may have gotten lucky in finding that article. But I expect to find out something different tomorrow. That picture doesn't match what I saw. I believe the ghost is *not* named Rose Stevens—Oh!" Her eyes popped open, and a shudder ran through her body. It was the best acting I'd seen from her yet.

Then I noticed Tania's satisfied smirk. I edged closer

to her as Madame Natasha started trembling. "What's happening," I whispered.

Tania grinned. "Rose heard her name, and she doesn't like Madame Natasha saying it's not true. Rose understands that much, anyway!"

The psychic spun around and looked wildly in every direction. Clearly she couldn't see the ghost any more than I could. Bruce took Madame Natasha's arm. "Is everything all right—why, you're freezing!"

"A sudden chill," the psychic stammered. "A cold spot in the room. The ghost must have heard me talking and, and knew we were discussing her. She wanted me to know she's not Rose—Oh!" She gasped and shuddered. "I mean, she is . . . she may be . . ."

Mom wedged herself between Bruce and the psychic. "I think Madame Natasha should go up to her room. Perhaps get in bed and warm up. We'll have room service send up some hot tea."

She led Madame Natasha away. Bruce stared after them. "Amazing! That woman really has the gift. I must persuade her to come along for some of our other shows."

Tania looked at me and rolled her eyes. I shrugged. She was the one who wanted to keep her ghost sighting a secret.

Bruce looked around at the TV crew and glanced at

his watch. "All right, everyone, dinner break. Let's pack it up for the night. I want to get an early start tomorrow, though. We'll be filming when Madame Natasha tries to talk to the ghost. Maggie, make sure you get that camera working." He turned to Tania. "Thanks for the article, honey. Maybe we will be able to use it. Let me go up and get this makeup off. Do you kids want to go ahead into dinner?"

"Of course," I said.

"We'll see you in there," Tania said.

Bruce bustled up the stairs. The rest of the crew started packing up cameras and things.

"So what exactly happened," I asked.

"The ghost—Rose—started paying attention when we said her name. She came down the stairs. It made me so mad when that fraud babbled about how she could see the ghost, and it wasn't Rose. I guess it made Rose mad too. She reached out for Madame Natasha." Tania laughed. "She didn't know what hit her!"

"Yeah, I guess she *can* recognize a ghost, when one reaches out and grabs her." My stomach grumbled. "Let's go in to dinner."

"Just a minute. I want to talk to Rose, once these people get out of here."

Maggie went past us carrying a big black box. She smiled and said, "Hey!"

"Hey!" I croaked back, turning to watch her walk down the hallway. The rest of the crew followed, or went up the stairs. The two desk clerks were busy arguing about Madame Natasha's strange behavior.

I glanced at them and said, "We won't get a better chance."

Tania nodded. "Let's see if we can lead her back up the stairs, out of sight." She led the way, darting a quick glance to the side. "Rose! Rose, come with us."

I trailed after, trying not to step where the ghost might be. I had that weird sensation of hearing only half a conversation. I wondered if it was like that for movie actors, in a scene where special effect monsters will be added later.

Tania stopped partway up the steps, where the banister hid us from the desk clerks. I stopped a few steps farther down.

"Rose," Tania said. "We have to talk to you. We found out something about what happened. We know you're upset because your husband never came back, because you think he abandoned you. But we don't think that's true. We think he died. It must have been within a few—"

She stopped and drew back, her face white with shock. "Wait, Rose, don't, it's not that bad! He loved you, I'm sure he did."

"What's going on?" I demanded.

"She's really upset. I guess she didn't realize that Frank must've died by now."

"It's been over a hundred years!"

"Not to her."

"But what's she doing?"

"She just kind of collapsed, and she's crying. Oh, I feel so bad!" Tania knelt and reached forward.

"Don't touch her!" I yelled.

"What on earth are you two doing?"

Tania and I froze, and slowly turned to see Maggie at the bottom of the stairs.

CHAPTER 20

My mind went blank. I could only stare at Maggie and feel the color rise in my face.

"It was, um, it was . . . a mouse," Tania stammered.

"A mouse." Maggie came up the stairs to join us. We all looked around for the nonexistent mouse. I said lamely, "It's gone now."

"I can see that."

"But, you know, mice can carry disease, and I didn't want Tania to touch it."

Maggie looked like she was trying not to laugh. "Good for you. But I'm curious, Jon. You said don't touch *her*. What made you so sure the mouse was female?"

I stared at her. "Um . . . it looked like a girl mouse?"

"Uh-huh."

"It did!" Tania said. "It had these really long eye-lashes, like a cartoon mouse when they want to show it's a girl."

Maggie and I both turned to stare at her. Tania gave this little shrug, grinned, and said, "But she wasn't wearing a bow."

"I see." Maggie was definitely trying not to laugh. "I'll be sure to mention to the hotel that they have a mouse problem." She went on up the stairs, turned at the top, and gave a little wave. "See you later."

Tania and I didn't speak again until we were seated in the restaurant and the waiter had brought water and bread sticks.

"That was awful," Tania said. "I'm sorry, Jon. I know how much you like her."

"I don't like her that much," I said, blushing furiously. "I mean, she's nice and all, but . . . it's no big deal."

Tania grinned. "Right. Here, you can have my bread stick." She sighed. "I like her too. I wish we could tell her. It would help to have someone, you know, grown up, knowing what's going on."

"Well, we can't. She'd just think we were making up stories and being childish."

"A fate worse than death?" Tania quipped. She put her fingertips to her temples and gazed somewhere above my head. In a fairly good imitation of Madame Natasha's voice, she said, "I foresee a future when Maggie joins the *real* ghost hunters. She'll be Velma to your Shaggy."

"Yeah, what does that make you, Scooby Doo?"

"Of course! He's the coolest of the gang."

We grinned at each other. "But back to the real question," Tania said. "What are we going to do about Frank and Rose?"

"I have no idea. If Rose can't handle the idea that Frank is dead, does it matter how or why he died?"

"But I can't just leave her here like this! She's so unhappy. And it could go on like this for years—centuries. Forever."

That was pretty sad. "Well, what else can we do? Visit the cemetery again?"

"I do want to find Rose McGloin's tombstone. Maybe it will tell us something."

I glanced out the window. The sky had turned dark and stormy again. It wasn't raining yet, but it sure looked like it planned to. I did my best Bruce voice. "It was a dark and stormy night . . . and ghosts walked the land." I reached for the last bread stick. "Tomorrow morning, then."

"We don't have much time. Can't we do anything tonight?"

"You really want to visit a cemetery at night?"

Tania stared at me, and I didn't like the considering look in her eyes. "That's a great idea."

I sighed. "Guess I'd better order a big dinner."

CHAPTER
21

How do I get myself into these things? I should have been up in my room watching movies on cable. Instead, I was sneaking into a cemetery in the dead of night. All right, so it was actually only about eight o'clock, but with the storm coming on, it felt like night. The sun had set, except for some sickly color low in the sky, like blood and dirt running down the drain from washing a wound.

The wind felt like it was trying to peel the hair from my head. Tania had pulled hers back, but loose strands whipped around her face.

"You know what's the worst thing?" I said. "If we get caught, they'll blame me for dragging you into this."

She smiled sweetly. "It must be hard to be you."

We stumbled up the rocky path. Of course, it had to be outside of town, on a hill with dark woods behind it. I had my flashlight, a mini Maglite that shone brightly on about one square foot of ground at a time. I really needed a big lantern. Or maybe a torch. Yeah, like the mad crowd storming Frankenstein's mansion. This was just as crazy. Heck, I wouldn't mind having that crowd here too, mad or not.

Lightning flashed, and a second later a boom shook the air. The lightning image stayed burned in my eyes: looming grave markers white against the dark trees. Some fancy stone monuments with angel wings and things on top were taller than I am. One big box must have been a crypt.

Tania stopped, so I did too. I said, "This is pretty spooky. Are you sure you want to do it now?"

She didn't answer. I looked down into her face and saw staring eyes and a trembling chin. Her hands were clenched by her side.

Drat. I'd forgotten about extra ghosts. "Um . . . can you see any ghosts here now?"

Her voice didn't shake too much when she said, "Not as many as you might expect."

You know when they talk about a chill going down your spine? Well that really happens. I looked around the cemetery, but I only saw graves. It was creepy enough. I couldn't decide which would be worse, seeing ghosts, or knowing they were there but not being able to see them. I wondered if I could start not believing in them again.

"So how many ghosts are we talking about here?"

Tania's lips moved as her eyes scanned the cemetery. "I see eight." She pointed to a section of newer-looking marble tombstones. "Most of them are over there."

"Are any of them coming this way?"

"Not yet. I guess either they don't know I can see them, or they don't care."

"How about pretending you don't see them? Maybe they won't figure it out, and we can get out of here without another close encounter of the ghost kind."

She glanced at me and shuddered. "Yeah, I think you're right."

I remembered Maggie talking about the amulets that Bruce had. I wished I had bothered to ask him about them, and had tried to get one for Tania. I wasn't sure I believed the amulets did anything, but I was finding myself more open-minded every minute.

"So now what?" I asked. I wanted to let Tania make the decision. And if she wanted to head back to the hotel, I was ready to go.

"We go back to the graves from the 1890s, I guess."

Darn. We walked past the nice clean tombstones. Tania had her head down, but she kept darting sideways glances. It reminded me of trying to hide from a scary movie but watch it at the same time. Since I couldn't see the ghosts anyway, I forced myself to study the tombstones.

The wind died down. The moon shone from behind some patchy clouds, but it was still hard to see. I pointed to the left. "Over there, right?"

Tania walked a few paces away and crouched. "This one's from 1901. Oh, she only lived a few months. Poor thing."

"Yeah. Um, she's not . . . still here, right?"

"No." Tania stood up and looked around. "I wonder why some people become ghosts and not others."

I shrugged. "You got me. Ask a ghost."

Tania edged closer. "Actually, I think we might have to do that."

"What do you mean? I thought we weren't going to talk to any of them." I hoped my sister hadn't decided that all these ghosts needed our help.

"Yes, but there's a man sitting on that log over there. I think he's watching us. And that's where the right age graves are. We're going to have to go over there."

I squinted, but saw only an old fallen tree in the gloom. Tania was right though, that was where we'd been earlier. "Well, does he look, um . . . mean?"

Tania peered toward the tree. "It's hard to tell from here. But he's sitting with his legs crossed."

I had to admit, that didn't sound real threatening. But the whole thing was still creepy.

Tania led the way closer. "Hey!" she hissed. "Look at what he's wearing."

"I can't! What is he wearing?"

"His suit looks old—I mean, it looks new, but it's old-fashioned. Like in those photos at the historical society. Maybe he's from the 1890s too."

"Wouldn't that be swell," I muttered. "Look, just ignore him, okay?"

Tania took a deep breath. "Right. Mom was looking at that row, right?" She led the way, darting glances over her shoulder.

"Ignore him," I muttered. Then I spoke louder, trying to shake off the creepy feeling with a brave voice and logical behavior. "All right, we're looking for Rose McGloin, died 1894. Shouldn't take long." I lowered my voice. "But let's stick together."

"Definitely," Tania whispered. She glanced back over her shoulder again, stumbled into me, and screamed.

CHAPTER 22

I shoved her behind me. "Get back!" I looked around wildly, my heart thundering. I tried to stay between Tania and where I thought the ghost was. I didn't know how to protect her from something I couldn't even see. "Just stay away from us!" I yelled.

I tried to use all my senses to feel the ghost. My eyes strained in the darkness but saw only shadows. My heart pounded so loudly, I couldn't hear anything else. I waited for a blow, or that unbearable coldness.

Nothing happened.

I felt Tania move behind me. She peeked around my arm. Then she squirmed out of my grasp and stepped out beside me.

"What are you doing?" I hissed.

"It's all right now. He just startled me when he ran over here so fast. He's sitting back down on that log now and he says he's sorry he scared us."

I was sorry too. My heart felt like it was going to break out of my chest. Can teenagers have heart attacks?

Tania started forward, but I grabbed her arm. "Wait. What makes you think we're safe now?"

She hesitated. "I don't know. He's not scary now. He's calmer than Rose."

That was real comforting.

Tania's gaze flew to the tree. "Yes, Rose McGloin."

"What?" I said. "Did he speak?"

She took a couple of steps forward. "I can, but my brother can't. How often can someone see you?"

She seemed to be listening. I grabbed her arm. "What? What's he saying?"

She turned to me and blinked a few times. "He says hardly anyone can see him, but it's most common with girls my age. Just like what I read. Isn't it funny!"

"Hysterical," I muttered. "Can we get on with this?"

She turned toward the tree. "We met Rose at the hotel. Her ghost, I mean. We're trying to find out what happened to Frank McGloin so we can tell her."

I stayed close by Tania's side as she stared at the tree. I guess she was listening. Then she turned to me, smiling. "We found him! Isn't that incredible?"

"What?" I almost screamed. "I can't hear what he's saying. You don't mean—"

"That's right," she said. "This ghost is Frank McGloin!"

CHAPTER 23

It seemed too good to be true. I glared at Tania. It was a pretty complex plot just to play a practical joke on her brother. "You don't really expect me to believe—"

"Just a minute," she said. She was listening again.

I waited, feeling foolish. "Tania," I hissed. "Tania!"

Finally she turned to me. "This is incredible. He's been waiting here all these years for Rose."

"What do you mean, waiting?"

"After they checked into the hotel, he went out for cigarettes. Only he got mistaken for a bandit and shot dead in the street. He says he wasn't the man they were looking for, but they drew on him before he had a chance to say anything. The next thing he knew, he was here. Isn't that sad?"

"Yeah, I've heard that cigarettes kill, but I didn't know it could happen so fast."

She gave me a push. "How can you joke about it? He can hear you, you know."

That was sort of embarrassing. Tania went on. "He says he was buried here under the wrong name. He felt awful about leaving his wife, but he didn't know what to do about it. Then, three days later, her body showed up when they buried her. But her ghost wasn't with it."

"Wait a minute," I said. "Do ghosts usually travel with their bodies?"

Tania turned back toward the tree. I guess the ghost really could hear me, because she didn't have to repeat my question. I waited for what seemed like an eternity, still wondering if this was some kind of joke.

Finally she said, "He says lots of people are ghosts for a few days. They can't believe at first that they're really dead. They hang around their graves for awhile, and then they accept it and move on. Those ghosts in the new section were all buried within the last month."

"Wait," I said. "Move on where?" That question had bothered me ever since Angela died and I'd had to listen to Mom and Dad disagree about life after death.

Tania turned toward the tree and whispered, "Where? Do you know where people go?" After a moment, she sighed and turned back to me. Her voice shook. "He doesn't know. He hasn't been there yet." She took a deep breath, and said more calmly, "He's been afraid to let go without knowing what happened to Rose."

I gulped hard and realized that for those few seconds I had believed, really believed, that Tania was talking to a ghost and I'd hoped he would have the answer. But answers don't come that easily.

I sighed. "All right, this is fantastic. We know what happened to the husband, and we even found him. So now what do we do?"

Tania walked closer to the fallen tree. I guess she wasn't afraid of this ghost at all. But I was still worried about what would happen if he tried to touch her.

"Look," Tania said to the tree, "we want to help, but I haven't been able to talk to your wife." She added apologetically, "She's, um . . . kind of emotional. She doesn't—she can't communicate the way you do."

After a long pause, she said, "Yes, I guess that's what happened."

"What?" I asked. "What did he say?"

"He said Rose always was sensitive."

I almost laughed. That wasn't the word that came to my mind from Tania's descriptions.

"And he said he's seen that with other ghosts who haven't been able to move on. If they're really angry or upset about something when they die, they get less human over time. It's like the emotion takes over everything. That must have happened to Rose. Only she got stuck at the hotel, because that's where she was waiting when she was alive. And she's still waiting."

"Okay, great, so what do we do?" I just didn't get all this ghost stuff.

Tania listened, then turned to me with a frown. "He says he tried to go into town to look for Rose after her funeral, but he couldn't get very far from the cemetery. But he's willing to try again."

"All right, so we bring a ghost back to the hotel. Bruce would be proud, if only he knew."

It was so weird, walking back through the cemetery at night knowing—or at least sort of believing—that a ghost was walking with us. Tania made small talk, answering questions about us. I remembered Mom and Dad always telling us not to talk to strangers. Is it better or worse if the stranger is a ghost?

It started to drizzle. With the moon hidden, it was so dark, I could hardly see Tania. I wondered if darkness made a difference in how well she could see the ghost, but it seemed rude to ask, with him right there.

We left the cemetery and started down the path toward town. Then Tania stopped and said, "Uh-oh."

"What's happening now?" I asked.

"Frank's getting stuck."

"What do you mean, stuck?"

"He's trying to come with us," she said, "but he says it's like . . . like he's separating from his body."

"He's already separate from his body."

"All right, his spirit then, his ghost, whatever." She paused. "He says it's like he's peeling away from his soul. Frank, you'd better stay here. It won't help Rose if this destroys you." They talked for a few minutes, while I stared into the darkness, wondering if I was the one going crazy. Was I a fool for believing Tania, or for doubting her? I really didn't need this kind of confusion in my life.

"I guess we'll go back to the hotel without him," Tania said. "We can't do anything more here. I'll have to find a way to communicate with Rose."

I sighed. No, answers never came easily. Not to any of the important questions. "All right. Bye, Frank." I turned my collar up against the rain, and we walked back to the haunted hotel.

CHAPTER
24

"Jon! Jon!"

I was dreaming about Maggie, sitting on a tombstone eating ice cream, and lecturing me about how only fools believe in ghosts while hundreds of spirits straight out of a cartoon flew around her head.

"Jon!"

"Mmph. What?"

Tania was shaking me. I groaned and sat up. I blinked at the clock: 4:42 in the morning. Other than the digital light, I couldn't see a thing in the room. I fumbled for the lamp and switched it on. "What's wrong? What happened?"

"I think I know how to move Rose."

I rubbed my eyes. "What are you talking about?" Tania was dressed, and carrying her coat. I had a feeling I wasn't going to like this.

She stared down at me. "I think . . . I think I can take her inside myself. I just have to let her—"

"No! She'll kill you. Just look what's been happening—she touches you, and you get cold and sick. You need to stay away from her, not get closer."

Tania perched on the edge of the bed. "I told you, she doesn't mean to hurt me."

"I don't care what she means! This is crazy."

Tania's jaw jutted forward. "It's the only way. Rose can't move away from this place on her own. But we already have a connection, and if I just let us connect all the way, she can move with me. I'm sure of it!"

"How sure?"

Her gaze wavered, and dropped to her lap. "Pretty sure."

I rubbed my hands over my face. It was too much to ask me to think clearly this early in the morning. But I didn't need the sharpest mind to know that this was a very bad idea.

"Look, Tania, can we talk about this later?" Maybe she would come to her senses. Maybe we wouldn't have time for ghost transportation once everybody else was up and busy.

She scowled. "No. We have to do it now! People will be up soon, and that will make it harder. What if

Mom wants to spend more time with us? And they're supposed to finish filming today, so we might leave. It's now or never."

Drat. She figured it out.

I sighed. "Tania, you can't expect me to do this. It's too dangerous for you. What would Mom say if I have to tell her that her only remaining daughter went crazy because she was possessed by a hysterical ghost?"

Tania was trembling, but she stared straight at me. "If you don't help, I'll do it alone. I'm not going to leave Rose here like this."

I considered my options. I could tie up Tania with the curtain cords, but that would cause another kind of trouble. I could run for help, but they would just think I was the crazy one. And Tania would probably manage to slip away to get Rose on her own.

I didn't have too many choices. If Tania was determined enough, she'd find a way to do this. The best thing I could do was help her, so she didn't get into even more trouble.

I groaned and slipped out of bed. "All right. Let's go get a ghost."

CHAPTER
25

Tania squealed and threw her arms around me. "I knew you'd help!"

"Give me a minute to get dressed."

She danced out of the room and closed the door behind her. I fumbled into my jeans and T-shirt. I pulled on a sweatshirt and my jacket and stuck the flashlight in my pocket. As I laced up my sneakers, I started a mental list of things to always keep on hand in case of supernatural encounters or demanding little sisters. *Big* flashlight, gloves, a warm hat, good hiking boots, a first-aid kit—though I wasn't sure what kind of first aid you did for a ghost freezing. Maybe one of those foil thermal blankets?

I remembered the amulets again. Was there any way we could get one, or all of them?

Did Bruce have the amulets here, or did he leave them back at the studio, or at his house? If he did have them here, where would they be? In his hotel room?

I wasn't about to go knocking on his door at this time of the morning, asking to see them. It would be suspicious, for one thing. For another, he was in there with my mother, and that was something I didn't even want to think about too closely.

When my parents first split up, Dad moved out and we lived with Mom. But when Mom married Bruce, and took the job on his show, she would have to travel too much. Dad moved back into our house, and Mom moved in with Bruce. So I didn't have to witness my mother sharing a bedroom with another man, and I wanted to keep it that way.

Finally I couldn't put it off anymore. I opened the bedroom door to find Tania in the living room fidgeting like a caffeinated hummingbird.

Tania started for the door, but I grabbed her arm. "Hold on. Can this wait just a couple of hours? I really want to get one of those amulets Maggie told us about."

"The ones for exorcisms? We're not trying to exorcise her. We're trying to help her."

"Look, I'll take any kind of protection we can get. Humor me, all right?"

She hesitated. "But I don't want to wait. I want to go right now. I'm afraid if I wait, I'll . . ." She glanced into

146

my eyes and then away. "I'm afraid I'll lose my nerve."

That was another good reason to wait, in my opinion. But I just said, "It won't be long. It's almost five now. You know how Mom talks about working from dawn to dusk on these shoots, because it's so expensive to be on location."

"But it will be harder to get Rose out with people around. I don't want to have to talk to Mom while Rose is inside me."

Good point. I ran my hands through my hair. "All right, let's just think for a minute." Where would Bruce keep the amulets, if he had them at the hotel? I snapped my fingers. "Hey, what about the prop room! Didn't they get a room just for all the equipment?"

"Yeah, I think so. Not a hotel room, but they're using one of the meeting rooms on the ground floor so they don't have to haul things in and out every day."

"So if Bruce brought the amulets, and the amulets are equipment, sort of, they might be in there."

Tania grinned at me. "It's worth a try. But it will be locked, won't it, with all that expensive stuff in there?"

I shrugged. "Let's find out." I added a lock pick to my list of necessary items. I wondered where you got one, and how you learned to use it.

I led Tania toward the back stairs. "Remember," I said, "keep away from the ghost, until we have an amulet."

"Would you please call her Rose," Tania said. "She's a person."

"Not anymore."

I could hear faint sounds from around the hotel—creaks and groans that, I told myself, were just the old building settling. We crept down the hall. We didn't really need to creep. No one was around, and even if they were, we weren't doing anything wrong. But we couldn't help ourselves—we crept.

When we got near the lobby, I whispered, "We'll have to go past the desk clerk. We'd better act like we know where we're going."

Tania considered a moment. "But we don't. And it will look worse if we have to come back and ask questions." She peeked around the corner. "It's the woman who was here when we arrived. Let's just go talk to her." She started forward before I could answer.

Was it the same woman? I hadn't paid attention at the time, but Tania greeted her like an old friend. "Good morning! How are you?"

The clerk smiled at her. "Just fine. You're up early this morning."

Tania nodded. "Bruce—that's my stepfather, the one in charge of the show? He asked us to get something from the prop room, only we're not sure which room it is, so he said to just ask you."

"It's down the hall," she said, pointing, "the second door on the left. Do you have a key?"

"Oh!" Tania's cry of surprised regret was so sincere, I almost believed her. "He forgot to give it to us." She half-turned away from the counter, as if she were about to go back upstairs. Then she paused and said, "But he'll be in the shower now. I don't want to disturb him. I don't suppose you could—" She shook her head. "Never mind. I guess we'll just have to wait. He'll understand." She gave the woman a worried look, and you could easily believe that Bruce would yell at her or worse if she didn't do what he'd asked.

"Now don't you worry," the woman said quickly. "Seeing that you're his stepdaughter and all, I guess I can let you in." She smiled at Tania, and then looked at me.

I gave her my friendliest smile. "We're just, you know, trying to be helpful."

She immediately frowned and said suspiciously, "Yes, well, I'll have to go with you and wait while you're in there."

Man, why is it Tania can tell a pack of lies and everyone thinks she's the sweetest thing who ever lived. I say one thing that's basically true, and they think I'm a juvenile delinquent.

The woman picked up a set of keys and led the way

down the hall. As we trailed behind her, I whispered to Tania, "You should be an actress." She smiled until I added, "Or a politician."

She wrinkled her nose at me. "Well, you should say as little as possible, because if you can't be more subtle, you'll never get away with anything."

I couldn't argue. Story of my life.

The desk clerk unlocked the door and stepped aside. We walked past her into a small room crammed with tripods, camera cases, and all kinds of boxes. Tania glanced back at the woman and smiled. Then she whispered to me, "This place is worse than your room! What are we looking for, anyway?"

I shrugged. "Your guess is as good as mine." We wandered slowly among the boxes, trying to read labels. What would someone do with a bunch of amulets? I tried to put myself in Bruce's mind, horrible as that was. "Okay," I said quietly, "we have to remember that Bruce really believes in this supernatural stuff."

Tania shot me a look. "And you don't?"

Oh, right. I let that pass. "I mean, it's his life. He's probably spent years collecting these things, so he'd put them someplace special, like a fancy box, don't you think?"

Tania nodded. "But it could still be in one of these other boxes, or even in one of those black cases. I figured they'd just be camera equipment, but maybe that's not true."

The clerk called from the doorway, "What exactly are you looking for?"

My mind scrambled for an answer. "Uh, Bruce told us what the box looked like, but we didn't realize how much stuff there would be in here."

Amazingly, the vague answer seemed to satisfy the clerk. Tania turned so the woman couldn't see her, raised her eyebrows, and gave me a nod of respect. I grinned and went back to looking.

The more I thought about it, the more I decided Bruce wouldn't just have a cardboard box with a bunch of amulets jumbled inside. He'd have a fancy display case, with everything padded. It probably wasn't too big, though—maybe the size of a briefcase. I stood in the middle of the room and turned slowly, scanning every item.

"There!" I pointed at a dark wooden box, a little larger than a briefcase, sitting on a stack of black and silver equipment cases.

Tania stood on her toes trying to see. "Where?"

I reached up and pulled down the box, hoping I was right. The clerk would get suspicious if we kept searching different boxes.

I set the box on a case in the corner so the woman

wouldn't be able to see what we were doing. I was relieved when the latch popped open without a key. Tania stood next to me and we gazed down at more than a dozen amulets resting in silk padding. Some were crosses, and others looked like words in foreign writing. I saw an eye, an elephant, a turtle, and even a beetle. Smaller amulets and some little bells were fastened to the inside of the lid.

Tania pulled up on a fabric tab along one side of the box. "Look, it's just a tray. There are more underneath."

We glanced at each other. We couldn't take all of them. Someone would notice if we carried the whole case out of the hotel and back.

Tania said, "We should take one from the lower level, in case someone opens the box."

I lifted out the top tray. Tania stared at the amulets underneath. "So which one?" she asked.

"I don't know. You're the one who's psychic or whatever. Close your eyes and pick one. Listen to your heart or your soul or something."

Tania glared at me for a second, then closed her eyes tightly and took a deep breath. I made sure I was blocking the clerk's view as Tania's hand hovered over the case. Then it came down and landed on a five-inch-tall silver cross. She opened her eyes and looked at it.

We shrugged at each other. Tania slipped the cross into her jacket pocket.

Tania walked toward the door, saying cheerfully, "Sorry to keep you waiting! We've got it now."

I glanced over my shoulder, then reached in and grabbed a silver four-leaf clover, a horseshoe, and something that looked like a wheel. I figured it couldn't hurt. I shoved them in my pocket, then put the top tray back in, closed the case, and put it back on the stack of boxes.

We thanked the desk clerk and hurried away while she was locking the door. We stepped out into the lobby. "Wait," I said. "If the clerk sees us go outside, she'll know we didn't take anything to Bruce. And if she sees you talking to Rose, it'll look really weird." I could already hear her footsteps behind us. I hurried Tania forward. "Let's go up the elevator. She'll think we're going to Bruce's room. We can come around from the back and meet up with the ghost at the top of the stairs. You do . . . whatever it is you think you can do, and then we just have to get out of the building."

Tania nodded. "Good plan."

CHAPTER
26

We got in the elevator and Tania waved at the desk clerk as the doors closed. The elevator rose with a *whoosh* that made my stomach feel empty. When we got to the top, I dragged Tania to the far end of the hall.

"Where are we going?" she asked.

I pulled her into a little room with a soda machine and ice maker. "Good, you're wearing a chain. Put the amulet on it."

Tania pulled out the amulet and frowned at it. "It will look ridiculous on this little necklace."

"Hopefully no one will see it. Tuck it into your shirt and zip up your jacket."

When she had that amulet in place, I pulled the others out of my pocket. It was hard to believe they would actually do anything, but then it was hard to believe any of this. "Take these, too."

Tania giggled as she tucked the amulets into different pockets. "All right. Can we go now? I feel well protected."

I was glad one of us was happy. I didn't like any of this. If something happened to Tania—I couldn't even think about that. I just had to make sure nothing did.

The hallway had lights every ten feet, but it still seemed gloomy. Or maybe it was just my mood. I could hear Tania breathing too quickly. "This will work," I said. "No problem at all."

She gave me a quick smile. But maybe I shouldn't comfort her. Maybe I should try to scare her, so she'd give up. But what would happen then, if we just left, without ever finishing this?

When we neared the end of the hallway, I put out an arm to stop her. I looked down into her face. I wanted to ask, "Are you sure about this? Do you know what you're doing?" Instead I said, "Are you ready?"

She set her jaw and nodded. We turned toward the top of the stairs. The stairway was empty, at least to me. A murmur of voices came from the desk below.

"Tell me what you see," I whispered.

"She just appeared," Tania said. "Like she was waiting for us."

"Now what?"

Tania turned toward the top of the stairs and said

softly, "Rose, you have to come with us. We're going to take you to Frank." She held out her hands. "You can do it. Just come with me."

My whole body tensed, waiting for something—I didn't know what.

Tania's hands twitched, and she whimpered. Tears wet her eyes, but she gave a shaky smile and murmured, "That's it."

Tania moaned. Her eyes half closed, and she swayed. I grabbed her to keep her from falling. We were both bundled in coats, but I could feel the cold radiating from her.

Tania gasped and opened her eyes. She shivered violently for several seconds, but then the shaking stopped and she took a few deep breaths. She smiled weakly at me, but her eyes seemed unfocused. I held her arms tightly, wanting to shake the ghost out of her or drag her away.

"We did it," she mumbled.

"You got her? She's—inside you?"

"Yes." She put a hand to her chest, and hunched her shoulders around it. "Let's go—quickly," she gasped. "So much—hurt."

I hurried her down the stairs. It would take at least ten minutes to get to the cemetery, if we ran. If Tania could run.

At the bottom of the stairs, I glanced toward the

check-in desk and nearly tripped on the smooth carpet. I recognized that broad back and highlighted blond hair. Bruce was talking to the desk clerk.

I held my breath, gripped Tania's arm, and tried to move silently across the lobby.

I reached out for the doors. Almost there.

"Kids!" Bruce called out.

I grimaced at Tania, but she was staring straight ahead and didn't seem to see. Even Bruce would have to notice that something was wrong with her. I turned to him with a big fake grin. "Um, good morning! We were just going out for a walk."

He bounced over to us. I tried to keep between him and Tania as I fumbled for the door.

"Don't run off yet," he said. "Why don't you join us for breakfast?"

"Um, no thanks, we're not really, um—" Wait a minute—us?

Sure enough, when I looked around the stairs, I saw Mom hurrying toward us. Maggie waved from a bench. Man, didn't these people ever sleep?

Mom gave me a kiss on the cheek. "I never thought I'd see you up this early!" She started messing with my hair. I squirmed and glanced at Maggie. Her smile was full of laughter. I realized I hadn't showered or combed my hair or anything.

Tania hadn't even turned from the door. She just stood rigid, waiting.

Mom moved over to hug her, but it looked awkward because Tania didn't hug back. Mom said, "How are you feeling this morning? Are you sure you should be running around this early?" She frowned and peered into Tania's face.

I tried to step between them. "Uh, she had a bad dream. We're just going for a walk to forget about it."

"But it's still dark outside!" Mom exclaimed. "And chilly." She rubbed Tania's arms through her coat. "Darling, you're already frozen."

Tania's face twisted with pain. She mumbled, "Frank."

I was practically dancing a jig, trying to get Mom to look at me instead. "That's why we're, uh, going jogging! To warm up."

Mom's brow furrowed. "Jogging at six o'clock in the morning? I never thought I'd hear that coming from you. Are you sure you wouldn't like a hot breakfast instead?" She smiled and glanced at Bruce. "We always get an early start when we're on location, but I didn't expect to see you until at least nine."

"You won't!" I said. "I mean, we'll stay out of your way until nine. You get your work done. We don't want to interrupt." Tania swayed, and I heard a soft moan.

Maggie was walking closer, her eyes steady on Tania. "You guys want some company?" she asked.

"No!" I couldn't believe I was saying that, but I had to get us out of there fast, and alone. "I mean, maybe later. Right now we just want to get some fresh air."

I grabbed Tania, pushed open the door, and hustled outside. Tania stumbled alongside me as I dragged her down the big driveway. I didn't dare look back at the hotel. They had to know something strange was going on, and I could only hope they didn't try to follow us.

We reached the end of the driveway and I turned down the road out of town. Tania moaned and went limp. I wrapped my arms around her, trying to keep her from hitting the ground. Her head tossed and she flailed weakly, mumbling, "Jon! Help. Frank. Oh, Frank."

To anyone watching, it must have looked like we were either wrestling or cuddling. I was glad it was still dark out.

"Come on, Tania." I shook her gently. "Stay with me. We just have to go a little farther."

I propped her on her feet. She was sobbing, but she stayed upright. I put my arm around her waist. We staggered down the road, with Tania crying and mumbling. Right then I hated all ghosts, and Rose in particular. "I hope you're worth it," I muttered.

CHAPTER
27

I don't know how long the walk took. I'd forgotten to put on my watch. It felt like hours, but the sun wasn't up yet when we got there. I could just see a faint gray light back in the direction of town. I don't think Tania saw anything.

It was like Rose's personality—or what was left of it after a hundred years of misery—just took over. I couldn't get a sensible word out of Tania. Nothing but shuddering breaths and chattering teeth. By the time we reached the cemetery, my hand was numb just from supporting her. I guess the amulets were useless. Or maybe it would have been even worse without them.

I hauled her through the gate and past tombstones. "Frank!" I yelled. "Frank, get over here right now."

It hit me that I wouldn't know if he did appear, or be able to hear anything he said. I'd heard the phrase "the blind leading the blind." I was both blind and deaf, trying to lead someone who could see and hear, but couldn't communicate. What a mess.

I hoped Tania was still somewhere in her body, able to help Rose get out. But what if Rose didn't want to go? What if, after a century as a crying ghost, she decided getting a new body was better than moving on?

"Frank!" I screamed. "Come get your wife."

A chill passed through me, and I shivered. Was that Frank, trying to tell me he was here? Or was Tania getting even colder?

I threw Tania over my shoulder and staggered the last few yards to the fallen tree where she'd seen Frank's ghost. I set her on the thick trunk and held her upright. "All right, Tania, do your thing. Frank is here, and Rose is here, so let her go."

She stared, but I don't think she saw me.

"Come on, Rose," I said. "Come out of there. It's time to go."

Nothing happened. I wouldn't be able to see Rose, of course, but I could see that Tania wasn't back to herself.

"Tania!" I shouted. "What am I supposed to do?"

I leaned in so I was just inches from her face and I stared into her eyes. "Tania, you have to speak to me. Tell me what's going on. How can I help?"

She took a deep shuddering breath. "Here. Frank here. How . . . do I . . . let go? Where's—where am I?"

I wasn't sure if it was Tania talking, or Rose, or some of each. "You're here in the cemetery, with Frank. With me. Rose, you need to come out of Tania. You two need to let go of each other."

Tania looked around. "Where am I?" she repeated.

Couldn't she see? "You're here in the cemetery," I said. "You're here with Frank and me, and—" I glanced around at all the tombstones. Tombstones marking graves. Graves with dead bodies. I swallowed. "And you're here someplace too, Rose. You're buried here."

Tania gazed into my face. "Where? Where am I?"

I took a deep breath. "Let's find out."

I looked around at the markers, some of them cracked or covered with moss. Which one would be Rose's?

My gaze settled on a large pale tombstone with a fancy angel on top, its wings sweeping wide. I remembered Mom standing by it when she made her map. Rose's family had been rich, and she'd died too young, in tragedy.

I slipped my arms around Tania's waist and hoisted her up. "Come on, you two. Sorry, Frank—you three. Let's take a look."

I helped Tania over to the fancy tombstone. The sky had lightened enough to see pretty well. We knelt in front of it, and I read it aloud.

"'Rose McGloin. 1872 to 1894. Beloved daughter

and wife.'" I wondered who had written that. Someone who had wanted to erase the memory of Rose's abandonment, of her breakdown and tragic death? Well, it turns out they got it right.

Tania gasped. She tossed her head and moaned.

She slumped against me and lay still.

I rubbed her back through her coat. How long could someone stand being so cold? I tried to remember what to do for hypothermia. Get the victim warm. Yeah, right.

I could hear my heartbeat, counting off the seconds. One, two, three . . . an eternity in seconds.

Tania sat up and blinked. I could see in her face that she was herself again. Wherever Rose was, she wasn't inside my sister.

Tania shivered violently and rubbed her hands together. She seemed to be looking just above the tombstone. "Oh!"

"What is it?" I asked. "What do you see?"

"We did it! They're together."

"You did it," I said. "I just watched."

She smiled and shook her head at me. She addressed the air above the tombstone. "It's all right, then? Yes. I'm glad." She sighed. "I wish you could see them, Jon. They look so happy now."

"That's great." I wondered if Rose was sane again, but didn't ask.

"They can let go now," Tania said. "They're ready to go on, and find out what happens next." She sounded wistful.

I swallowed the lump in my throat. "Tell them to send us a postcard, and let us know what it's like."

Tania laughed. "Frank says he will, if they can."

Tania watched for a few more minutes. The first rays of sunshine warmed her face. She looked like herself again, but she had to be different, after all this. I knew I was. I still wasn't sure I'd done anything right. But Tania looked happy, and that was something. And we knew a little more about the world than we had. Unless of course, it was all in her mind—

Nah, she didn't look crazy. Not anymore.

Tania sighed. "They're gone. I hope they're happy."

"After all that, they'd better be," I said, but I was smiling. "Are you ready to go now?"

She nodded and got up. Her eyes widened in surprise. "You know what? I'm starving!"

We laughed and started back to the no-longer-haunted hotel.

CHAPTER 28

I felt like I really had been jogging, for miles and miles, as we trudged up the long driveway. The hotel looked almost cheerful as the sun hit it.

"I just thought of something," I said. "Bruce is shooting that scene with Madame Natasha today."

"So?"

"So the ghost isn't here anymore. She can't make contact, even if she's for real."

Tania wrinkled her nose. "Somehow I have a feeling it won't make any difference. She'll put on a great show for Bruce. I just hope Rose convinced her to use the right name. Not that it matters so much, but it would be nice if they got that one thing right."

"Yeah, I guess so." I found myself smiling at the thought of Bruce getting all worked up over a fake-psychic's lies while Rose cuddled up with Frank at the cemetery.

I could see a shadow just inside as we approached the door. It opened and Maggie peeked out. "Good timing. They're going to start filming in a few minutes."

I figured I looked awful, unshowered, hair messed up, bloodshot eyes. I was too drained to care—much. We slipped inside to find the TV crew hard at work. The makeup artist fiddled with Bruce's hair while he frowned and shook a piece of equipment. "Maggie, are you sure this thing is working? I'm not getting any reading at all."

Maggie winked at us and ran off to help Bruce.

Mom hurried over to us. "Are you okay?"

"Yeah, we're great." I hugged her, and didn't even care that people were watching. When I backed up, Tania slipped into Mom's arms and rested her head on her shoulder.

Mom said, "I was worried when you left so quickly. I wanted to go after you, but Maggie said she'd keep an eye on you."

Uh-oh. I stared at Maggie as she took the equipment from Bruce. She glanced up and met my eyes. I jerked my gaze away. "So, um, did she go out after us?"

"Yes, she just got back a couple of minutes ago."

What had she seen? I avoided looking at her as she walked over with Bruce.

"There you are," Bruce said. "Where did you go this morning, anyway?"

I gestured vaguely toward the door. "Just for a walk."

"I saw you head up the hill," Maggie said. "There's nothing up there but the cemetery."

I forced myself to meet her eyes and raised an eyebrow. "What do you have against cemeteries? You find lots of interesting people there."

Bruce chuckled. "See any ghosts?"

I shook my head. "Bruce, Bruce. You know my opinion of ghosts. After all, I've never seen one."

He grinned. "You're young; there's still time. Keep an open mind."

Tania giggled and buried her face in Mom's shoulder.

Bruce said, "We'd better get back to work. Are you going to watch the filming? Should be a great segment!"

Tania and I exchanged glances. I shook my head. "I think we're more interested in breakfast right now."

Bruce laughed. "I guess I had similar priorities at your age. He reached out for Mom's hand. Mom let go of Tania and headed up the stairs with Bruce.

Maggie lingered. "Look," she said gently, "I just want you to know you can come to me if you want to talk, about anything. I do want to be your friend. I guess this whole situation is pretty strange for you, and sometimes tough."

I almost laughed. Maggie didn't know the half of it—I hoped.

Maggie frowned. "Honestly, I do remember what it was like to be your age. And I know you can't always tell your parents everything. So I'm going to promise you, if you ever need my help, or just want to talk, I'll be here, and I won't tell your mom or Bruce. Anything you tell me will be just between us."

Tania and I exchanged a smile. We wouldn't tell Maggie anything yet. But maybe someday. Who knew—maybe she would even understand.

For now, I was just glad Tania and I had survived the night. We'd helped two people accept their deaths and move on to whatever happens next. That wasn't too bad.

Maggie was still watching us. I said, "Thanks. But we're okay right now."

Tania nodded. She looked tired, but she was smiling.

"Are you sure there isn't anything I can do?" Maggie asked.

I glanced at Tania, then grinned at Maggie. "Well," I said, "if you really want to, you could buy us breakfast!"

Maggie chuckled. "I could do that." She picked up a briefcase from the bench and led the way toward the restaurant. "And if you're curious, I can tell you about our next stop. I even have brochures in here. How do you feel about a steamboat trip? And guess what: It's supposed to be haunted."

Tania's eyes were bright with interest. "Really?" She hurried after Maggie. "What kind of ghost?"

I stopped, put my hands over my face, and groaned. Why couldn't I have a normal sister? Why couldn't I have a normal life?

I shrugged and followed them. Maggie already had brochures out as I sat down. Tania said, "And he's still trying to warn people about the disaster?"

I found myself grinning. Maybe normal was over-rated. With a sister who sees ghosts, life was sure to be interesting.

CHECK OUT SOME OTHER GHOSTLY BOOKS FROM ALADDIN:

From Aladdin
Published by Simon & Schuster